Breakdown in Axeblade

Frank and Joe inched along the narrow ledge of the cliff. All of a sudden the quiet of the hot early afternoon changed.

The *whupp-whupp-whupp* Frank had heard so faintly turned into a loud pounding sound, as a helicopter swooped down from above. The wind from its whirling rotors kicked up dust that stung Frank's face as he clung to the side of the mountain.

"Come on, Frank!" Joe called above the noise. "We've got to get out of here!"

Frank started moving again, slowly, scraping his feet along the ledge toward his brother.

Joe, watching the helicopter, saw the door slide open. His heart raced. The pilot leaned out of the chopper with a pistol in his hand!

The Hardy Boys Mystery Stories

Available from MINSTREL Books

The
HARDY BOYS®

BREAKDOWN IN AXEBLADE

FRANKLIN W. DIXON

PUBLISHED BY POCKET BOOKS

New York   London   Toronto   Sydney   Tokyo

A MINSTREL PAPERBACK *ORIGINAL*

 A Minstrel Book published by
POCKET BOOKS, a division of Simon & Schuster Inc.
1230 Avenue of the Americas, New York, NY 10020

Copyright © 1989 by Simon & Schuster Inc.
Cover art copyright © 1989 Paul Bachem
Produced by Mega-Books of New York, Inc.

ISBN: 0-671-66311-9

First Minstrel Books printing February 1989

10 9 8 7 6 5 4 3 2 1

Printed in the U.S.A.

Contents

BREAKDOWN IN AXEBLADE

1 Unfriendly Welcome

"It's the water pump," said Joe Hardy, staring at the engine of the disabled blue van. The seventeen-year-old's blond hair stuck to his sweaty forehead as the sun beat down on him.

Frank Hardy, a year older and an inch taller than his brother, shook his head. "You're wrong," he said. "It has to be the fan belt."

"No way," said Joe. He lowered the hood of the engine compartment and slammed it shut. "The engine's overheating and making that high-pitched noise. That means it's the water pump. Trust me."

Frank soaked a bandanna with water from a canteen and then squeezed it over his head. " 'Trust me'?" He laughed. "That's what you've

1

said every step of this trip. Like 'Trust me—this is the best road to take. We'll really fly on this small no-frills road.' No frills, all right. No gas stations, no phones, no cars, no trucks, no help."

"You left out no fun," Joe said, trying to make a joke. "Pass the canteen—I'm dying."

Frank handed his brother the canteen. Joe didn't bother with the bandanna. He just poured water over his head.

"Watch it," Frank said. "Without water we could really die in this heat."

The two brothers looked around—and saw nothing but an empty, straight, two-lane road surrounded by flat, dry prairie with mountains in the distance. No buildings broke the flat surface. Even the shrubbery was sparse.

"If this isn't the middle of nowhere, it's a close second," Frank said.

"It's not the middle of nowhere. It's the middle of Wyoming," Joe said. "At least I think it is. Too bad we lost the map."

"It certainly isn't Bayport." Frank sighed.

Bayport was where they had started from—their hometown on the East Coast. Unlike the towns they'd seen in Wyoming, Bayport was a bustling city full of houses, businesses, and exciting things to do. The two young detectives had left almost a week before, driving cross-country to camp, hike, and climb in the national parks out west. The trip was a vacation they'd been planning for months, long before school let out.

Frank leaned against the van, then jerked upright when his arm touched the metal, hot from the afternoon sun. "Okay. I'm going to trust you once more," he said. "You're the tour guide. What should we do?"

"I think we should drive till the motor dies," Joe said. "We don't want to stay out here waiting, and it's too hot to walk."

"Assuming the van will start again."

"Trust me," Joe said.

Frank gave his brother a grin, and the two of them climbed back into the van. The engine started up right away—but so did the hissing sound in the radiator.

"The next town could be miles from here," Frank said. "We'd better take it slow."

Taking it slow meant that twenty minutes later, they were only ten miles down the road. But a small town was in sight. "Don't fail us now," Joe said, patting the van's dashboard and accelerating slightly.

The sign at the town limits was encouraging: Howdy, Stranger. Welcome to Axeblade. Population 300 Friendly People.

"Hope one of the three hundred is a mechanic who knows something about fan belts," Frank said.

"Water pumps," Joe corrected, and he added, "Did you notice those other signs? Off the road? Seems to be a national park over there."

Ten minutes later the Hardys' noisy van inched its way down the main street of Axeblade, past a row of small, old, one-story buildings with pale,

3

peeling paint. A few old men sat outside one store, leaning their chairs back against the wall.

Axeblade seemed to have only one of everything—one restaurant, one launderette, one bank, one drugstore, one motel, and finally, near the end of town, one garage—B & J's Garage.

Joe pulled in, passing the two dust-covered gas pumps, and stopped at the open door of the garage area. A young man came out of the garage, wiping his hands on a rag. He was blond, about twenty-one years old, with a round face underneath a greasy, dark blue cap. His yellow T-shirt had oil stains on it, along with a picture of a heavy-metal rock group. At his feet was a large, old, spotted dog.

"Hi! How's it going?" the mechanic said. He sounded friendly and gave Frank and Joe the feeling that he was glad to see some new faces. The dog plopped down on the ground, resting his head on his owner's cowboy boots.

"We've got a problem," Frank said, stepping out of the van.

"Let's take a look," the mechanic said.

Joe started up the engine again, and the mechanic lifted the hood.

He listened for a moment and shook his head. "You've got a problem, all right. Water pump's giving out."

Joe gave his brother an I-told-you-so look as he climbed down from the driver's seat.

"Looks like your fan belt's about shot, too," the mechanic added.

4

Frank grinned a so-there grin at Joe.

"Okay, that's the bad news," Joe said. "How about the good news? Can you fix it?"

The mechanic shook his head. "Fixing it would be easy if I had the parts. But I don't. Take me two or three days to get 'em."

"Two or three days?" Frank was clearly disappointed.

"Yeah. Sorry. I wish I could help you guys out. Where are you headed, anyway?"

"Camping trip," Joe said. "We wanted to hit four of the national parks."

The mechanic's face seemed to shut up tight, like a steel trap. "Well," he said slowly, not looking at the Hardys, "your best bet's probably trying a garage farther down the road." He leaned down, intent on rubbing the van's headlights with his greasy rag.

"Hey, I've got a great idea," Frank said to his brother. "Maybe Axeblade's not exactly where we planned to camp, but that's a national park outside of town, right? Let's camp out there while the van's getting fixed. What do you say?"

"You know," the mechanic said before Joe could answer, "you guys really should keep on driving. Next town's Lawton—only forty-five miles from here. Compared to Axeblade, it's a big town. Lots of garages and lots of parts. Bet you could get fixed up over there fast."

"Think the van would make it?" Joe asked.

"Sure." But the mechanic wouldn't meet Joe's eyes. Chances were good that they'd overheat the engine and ruin it if they tried to drive forty-five miles without a fan belt and water pump. He didn't know why the mechanic would lie, but Joe was pretty sure that's what he was doing.

"Frank, camping in the park sounds great," Joe said, ignoring the mechanic's advice and watching his face for a reaction.

"That's not a good idea," the mechanic said in a flat voice. His forehead began to bead with sweat, and he wiped it off with the back of his greasy hand.

"Why's that?" asked Joe.

The mechanic didn't answer. Instead he changed gears: "You know, if you guys can't afford the motel 'cause your money's thin or something, you could bunk at my place. It's not a palace, but it's got a roof," he added with a grin. He was so friendly that most people probably wouldn't have noticed that he had changed the subject.

But Frank and Joe Hardy weren't like most people. Their detective instincts were starting to pump. Why was this guy switching his attitude every two seconds? First he was friendly, then he tried to convince them to keep on driving, and now he wanted them to spend the night at his place. They eyed the mechanic suspiciously.

"Hey, what's the matter with me?" The mechanic laughed. "You guys don't even know me. I'm Bill Hunt," he said, holding out his hand.

"I'm Frank Hardy, and this is my brother, Joe," Frank said as he shook hands.

6

"So what do you say? Want to bunk at my place?" the mechanic asked.

"Thanks for the offer, Bill, but we came out west to do some camping," Joe said. "I want to smell pine needles and campfires, not my brother's feet in the next cot."

"But I told you that's not a good idea," Bill Hunt said.

"Yeah, twice. I've been keeping score," Joe said. "But you never said *why* camping out is such a bad idea."

Bill Hunt cleared his throat and lowered his voice. "Okay, I'll tell you. It's the bears."

"You mean the Chicago football team has a secret training camp here?" said Joe with a smile.

Bill Hunt laughed and shook his head. "I mean real bears. There've been reports about some mean ones attacking campers in the park—a lot of them, in fact. See, it's not safe."

"We're used to taking care of ourselves," Frank said.

"Hey, I'm serious, you guys," Bill Hunt said.

Maybe he was. But a few bears in the woods weren't going to keep the Hardys from camping out.

"So are we," Frank said. "We'll leave the van here. See if you can put a rush on the repairs," he added as he climbed into the van. He handed out to Joe their backpacks—already stocked with supplies—and sleeping bags.

When the equipment was securely strapped to

7

their backs, the Hardys hiked out of Axeblade, heading west.

About nine miles down the road, the landscape changed—flat grasslands merged into the dense forests of what appeared to be a vast national park. The Hardys entered the forest and walked half a mile north before they found a clearing in the woods. They made camp and built a large, snapping fire of tree twigs and limbs. Frank added a few pinecones to the fire for the sound and the smell.

By the time they stuck whole potatoes in the fire the sun was going down, and they were starved. Frank cooked hot dogs on sticks as darkness closed in on them.

"What do you think was going on with that guy at the garage?" Frank asked, poking the fire. "He seemed so friendly at first, then he got weird."

"I think he probably doesn't know beans about fixing our van and wanted us to beat it so we'd be someone else's problem," Joe said, taking a bite of a blackened hot dog.

After dinner, Joe pulled out a flat aluminum-foil pan of popcorn from his backpack. He held the pan over the fire, and as the corn popped the foil top of the pan began to balloon out.

"You really know how to rough it, don't you?" Frank said, teasing his brother.

"Popcorn and no cola—that's roughing it if you ask me," Joe said.

Frank laughed, leaning back on his rolled-up

sleeping bag. Then he said softly and casually, as if he were asking for the mustard, "Don't make any sudden moves. I think we're being watched."

Joe sat perfectly still for a minute, his eyes wide open. "If it's a bear," Joe whispered, "he'd better have his own popcorn. I'm not sharing."

The branches of a tree suddenly twisted and moved. Slowly Frank dug into his pack for a flashlight. When the branch moved again, Frank aimed the beam right at the sound.

Brown eyes reflected the bright light. And then Frank and Joe saw the intruder clearly.

"A deer," Joe whispered.

"A beauty," Frank said quietly.

Frank and Joe and the deer stared at one another as though each was captured by the other's eyes. And then, when Frank turned off the light, the lithe, tan animal leapt away gracefully.

After the animal had gone, the Hardys sat quietly, listening. The park was alive with the sounds of birds and crickets. Shadows in the darkness told them that animals were climbing trees or scurrying across the ground.

"See. There's nothing to worry about, big brother. I like Axeblade. The people are friendly. Even the deer are friendly," Joe said.

"And the bears are probably so friendly they'll bring us bowls of porridge in the morning," Frank joked. "Let's get some sleep."

The Hardys piled up the fire and built a ring

around it with rocks so the fire couldn't creep out during the night. Then they spread open their sleeping bags and climbed in.

Again the sounds of movement in the woods reminded them that they weren't alone. A coyote howled in the distance. In the moonlight, Joe saw the silhouette of an owl swooping silently from its perch on a tree.

"Good night," Frank said as he settled into his sleeping bag.

But before Joe could answer, the bushes around them shook again. All of a sudden five men wearing jeans and dark shirts jumped out of the woods. In the light of the campfire, Joe could see that the men carried long, heavy tree limbs. Each man had a ski mask covering his face.

"Get up," ordered a sandpaper voice with a Western accent.

Joe's heart was racing. The men came closer, their clubs poised in midair. Both Hardys felt helpless because they were lying on their backs, with their attackers towering over them.

"What do you want?" asked Joe. He and his brother scrambled to their feet.

"Just shut up. We'll do the talking," said another voice with a twangy accent.

Everything was happening too fast, and it was too unexpected. Frank and Joe had been ready for bears—not men with clubs! What did these men want? And was this why Bill Hunt had told the Hardys to steer clear of the national park?

"Now, we can do this the easy way or the hard

10

way," said the man with the gravelly voice. He had a paunchy stomach that hung over his belt. When he gave the signal, the four others quickly surrounded the Hardy brothers.

"The easy way sounds good to me," Frank said.

"No argument," Joe added.

One of the ski-masked men suddenly pushed Frank to the ground.

"Get out of Axeblade and don't come back," said the leader, kicking out the Hardys' campfire. "And I mean get out *now*."

Frank stood up and brushed the dirt off his knees. "Come on, what's going on here?" he asked.

"He wants an explanation," said one of the other men, whose jeans were torn down near his boots.

"You want an explanation, kid?" asked the hoarse-voiced leader. "Too bad. That's the hard way. Come on—let's explain it to 'em, boys."

The five men quickly closed in on Frank and Joe, swinging their clubs. Frank and Joe put their arms up, ready to protect themselves. But they were outnumbered. The men whipped at the Hardys' faces and legs with the thick branches. The Hardys dodged, but they couldn't evade every blow.

As one of the clubs came swinging at him Joe grabbed it and pulled one of the masked men toward him with a strong jerk. Then he gave the man a karate kick to the knees that sent him to the ground.

"You'll pay for that," the biggest man said. With one painful swing of his club, he knocked Joe right off his feet. A moment later, Joe felt another blow to his head.

"Wait . . . Why . . . ?" Joe moaned the words weakly. Then he blacked out.

The last thing Joe saw before he lost consciousness was the group of five men—closing in on his brother, Frank.

2 No Help in Sight

Joe Hardy had regained consciousness, but he stayed on the ground for a minute. It took that long for his head to clear and for his memory to put the picture back together. The woods . . . five burly men . . . ski masks on their faces . . . hitting him . . . and Frank surrounded!

"Frank!" Joe sat up quickly. "Frank!" he called again.

"Yeah," came the quiet answer. "I'm okay."

"What was that all about?" Joe asked, standing up.

Frank shook his head in bewilderment. Then he, too, stood up. His legs were shaky, and his head throbbed.

Suddenly Joe and Frank looked around. The

13

woods were gone. So was their camp, their fire, and all of their equipment. They had been taken out of the park and left in the dust at the side of a four-lane highway.

"What do we do now?" Joe asked, still feeling groggy.

"We walk," Frank said.

So they walked, although their feet already hurt from the nine-mile hike they had made earlier that day. About a half mile down the road they came to a sign.

"Oh, no. We've been going the wrong way," Frank said. "Axeblade is ten miles behind us!"

"Population three hundred friendly people," Joe added sarcastically.

Reluctantly they turned around and started back toward Axeblade.

After walking about an hour in the cool night air, they came to a crossroads where the four-lane road they were on intersected with a two-lane. A road sign there indicated that Axeblade was six miles south on the two-lane.

"What's that noise?" Frank asked as a low rumble sounded in the distance. The rumble grew louder and louder until the road began to vibrate under their feet. They froze, and then, suddenly, headlights and a roaring engine barreled over a hill, heading straight toward them.

Frank and Joe jumped off the road and crouched behind some dried bushes that were

14

growing in an otherwise empty field. From there they watched a convoy of five gleaming silver tanker trucks speed toward them.

"Look at us," Frank said as the tankers came near. "What are we hiding from?"

"I don't know," Joe called over the engine noise. Suddenly Joe ran out into the road and started waving his arms, trying to flag down one of the trucks. "Hey! We need a ride!" he shouted.

But the tankers didn't stop. They must have been going ninety miles an hour, because the draft almost knocked Joe down as they passed.

By the time the Hardys got back to Axeblade on foot, it was long past midnight. Except for the motel's neon sign and lights in the sheriff's office, the town was dark. But there was a bulb burning in Bill Hunt's garage. They decided to go there first.

"Wow, what happened to you two?" Bill Hunt said. He was standing in the garage door with a lug wrench in his hand. His spotted dog lay at his feet.

"You tell us," Joe snapped. "You ought to know."

"And while you're at it," Frank said calmly, petting the dog's head, "you can cut all the good-guy cowboy talk. That college ring you're wearing is from UCLA, which means you've graduated from a hotshot school in California. So stop playing games with us. What are you doing up at this hour, anyway?"

15

Bill Hunt's face changed abruptly, and the open, friendly smile was gone. "Couldn't sleep," he answered. "And okay, so I've gone to college in L.A. So maybe this is a phony accent I put on. Maybe I've just seen too many Western movies. So sue me," he said. He called his dog and then walked back into the garage, leaving the Hardys outside.

But Joe and Frank followed him inside, and Joe hopped up onto the hood of a white Mustang that was having its oil changed. "Let's talk," Joe said in a dead-serious voice.

"Talk about what?" Bill Hunt twisted his college ring on his finger.

"We've got lots to talk about," Joe said. "Five guys jumped us in the woods, and I'll tell you something—they weren't from the Welcome Wagon. They used us for batting practice."

"And you knew they were going to do it, didn't you?" Frank said. "You told us not to camp in the park. So how did you know? What's your connection? Who were those guys, and why do they want us out of Axeblade?"

Bill Hunt started working on the lug nuts of a car up on the rack. "What are you guys? Detectives or something?"

"You got it," said Joe. "And we don't give up on problems until they're solved."

"Look, I'm sorry you got roughed up. I tried to tell you," Bill Hunt said. "But all I'm going to say now is what I said this afternoon, and you can take it as advice or a warning or whatever you

16

want. Take your van and haul it over to the next town."

"Why?" Frank asked again.

"Just quit asking questions." Bill Hunt turned his back on them and started working on the car again. "You can use the men's room to wash up if you want."

"We don't want to wash up," Frank said. "We want the sheriff to see what we look like when we make our report."

The mechanic shook his head. "Big mistake," he muttered.

"What's that supposed to mean?" Frank asked.

"You're the detectives," Bill Hunt said. "You figure it out." He pulled the wheel off the car and sent the tire rolling across the floor until it hit the wall. Then he started turning out the lights. "I'm closing up," he said.

"Yeah, I'll bet," Joe said sarcastically. "Great timing."

"Come on," Frank said quietly to his brother. "Let's go."

"Real good idea," Bill Hunt said.

Frank and Joe left the garage and headed up the street.

Moments later they entered the sheriff's office, a single brightly lit room with metal desks and well-worn swivel chairs. In the far corner, a police radio on a table squawked white noise.

Sitting with his stocking feet up on a desktop and his back to the door was a man in a gray police officer's uniform. He was reading a Western paperback novel that was torn at the edges. Country music blared from the tinny speaker of a small transistor radio on his desk.

When the Hardys walked in, the officer put his feet down, but he didn't put the book away. He turned in his swivel chair to face the two teenagers. A man in his fifties, with gray hair and a black-and-gray mustache, he watched the Hardys over the top of his reading glasses.

"Howdy, fellas," he said.

"Hi. I'm Frank Hardy, and this is my brother, Joe. Is the sheriff here?"

"You're looking at him," said the officer. "Sheriff J. P. Arthur. What can I do you for? Say, that's your van down at Bill Hunt's garage, isn't it? Sure is a fancy one, fancy as a ten-dollar Sunday shirt." His eyes followed them, but his head didn't move.

"Yes, it is," Frank said. "Sheriff, we were attacked and beaten up tonight out in the national park."

The sheriff's eyebrows met in concern, and his mouth scrunched to the side. "You wave a red flag in front of a bull to get his attention. Well, you got mine. Tell me exactly when and where."

"A couple of hours ago," Joe said.

"We don't know exactly where," Frank added. "We were camping in the park, and these five men wearing ski masks jumped out of the bushes. They told us to get out of Axeblade, and then they knocked us out."

"Did you get a good look at any of them?" Sheriff Arthur asked without much interest. He

18

kept playing with a button on his shirt. "What did they look like?"

"We don't know," Joe answered sharply. "My brother just *told* you—they were wearing masks." His voice was rising, and he could feel his face getting hot—a typical Joe Hardy reaction.

"Okay, okay. Calm down, son. You're as nervous as a new bronc. Did anything get stolen?" the sheriff asked.

"Not money, but we don't know about the rest of our gear," Joe said. "They dumped us on a highway outside Axeblade."

"Uh-huh," said the sheriff.

"Shouldn't you be writing this down?" Frank asked politely. Frank was always calmer than his brother—until he had proof that something was wrong.

Sheriff Arthur smiled at the question. "You boys haven't given me anything to write down. You got no names, no descriptions, you don't know if anything was stolen or where your camp was."

"Look at us. Look at these bruises and the dirt stains on our shirts. How do you think we got this way?" Joe asked.

"For all I know, maybe you two got into a fight. I know how brothers can scrap with each other. Got a brother myself."

Frank was beginning to see what Bill Hunt had meant when he said going to the sheriff would be a big mistake.

19

"Come on, Joe," Frank said, pulling his brother's arm.

"Hey, boys. Keep out of trouble, okay? Folks in Axeblade don't like trouble." Those were Sheriff Arthur's last words before the Hardys went out the door.

Joe, totally frustrated, started to boil over when they got outside. "Why didn't we tell him we're detectives and we know the difference between good and bad police work?" he asked his brother.

Frank smiled. "He'll find out we're detectives soon enough," he said. "He needs evidence about those five guys—and that's what we've got to find. But not tonight. What do you say we get some sleep and start fresh tomorrow?"

Frank pointed two doors down the street toward the Axeblade Motel, with its buzzing neon sign.

"I'd say that was one of your better ideas, big brother," said Joe as they walked toward the dimly lit motel office.

The man behind the check-in desk wore thick glasses and had a pale, sleepy face. He was sipping cola from a two-liter bottle when the Hardys walked in.

A small rotating fan on the desk did nothing but push stale air around the small room.

"What happened to you two?" asked the clerk.

"You know how brothers fight," Joe said.

"We need a room with a hot shower," Frank said.

20

"Uh-huh," the clerk said automatically. "That'll be twenty dollars in advance, if you don't mind."

He pushed the registration book toward Frank, but the large notebook wouldn't slide across the countertop because the wood was so dirty and damp. Frank lifted it forward.

As Frank filled out the registration page the telephone rang, and the desk clerk caught up the receiver on the first ring.

"Howdy, Ben," he said cheerfully. Then his face got serious. He said a couple of uh-huhs into the phone, looking hard at Frank and Joe the whole time. Then he turned his back on them and mumbled something quietly into the receiver so Frank and Joe couldn't hear. After a few more uh-huhs, the clerk hung up the phone and faced the Hardys again.

He wiped his forehead and took a big gulp from his cola bottle.

"Uh, I made a mistake, boys—no rooms. I'm full up tonight," he said.

"You're kidding," Joe said.

But Frank didn't let the clerk answer. "I looked at your guest register while you were on the phone. Nobody's staying here tonight. The motel's empty."

"Late arrivals," the clerk said, sweating and looking out the window.

Joe grabbed the first thing he could find—a plastic souvenir back-scratcher—and smacked it on the registration desk. "It's got something to do with that phone call, doesn't it? Who was that on the phone? Who's Ben?" Joe demanded.

"You might try hitching to Lawton. They got rooms," the clerk said automatically, tearing up the page Frank had been filling out.

"How could we ever leave Axeblade? It's such a friendly town," Frank said bitterly as he and Joe walked out the door.

Outside, the cool night air struck Frank and Joe, chilling them after the closeness of the motel office. Shivering, they walked along the empty street, their heads full of questions. What was going on in Axeblade? Why did everyone want them to leave? And most importantly, who was behind it all? Who had phoned the motel?

Frank and Joe were too exhausted to think about answering the questions. They desperately needed some rest. So with nowhere else to stay, they walked back to Bill Hunt's garage, crawled into their van, and quickly fell asleep.

It seemed like only minutes later that Joe was nudging his brother awake. "Sun's up," he said as the early-morning sunlight fought its way through the van's muddy back window.

"Pretty day," Frank said. "Makes you feel good. Makes you feel hungry. Think we can get something to eat around here?"

"I don't see why not," Joe said. "I'll just flash my famous baby blues at the waitress, and she'll probably drop huge piles of flapjacks and syrup in our laps. Trust me."

"I'd like to see that act work in *this* town,"

Frank said, laughing at his brother as they headed out into the sunny street.

But at the Morning Glory Restaurant, the waitresses wouldn't even talk to them, let alone serve them breakfast. And at the drugstore, where Joe tried to buy a sticky bun, the clerk just walked away from them.

Joe threw his hands up in disgust. "It's a time warp. That's what this is," he said. "It's like we're not here. We don't exist."

"No, it's like we're here and we're *not supposed* to be," Frank replied.

"Hey, you two!"

A voice called to them from halfway down the street. When Frank and Joe turned, they saw an old man in a faded plaid Western shirt, wearing a ten-gallon hat. His mouth was hidden somewhere in his bushy beard.

"Is he really talking to us?" Joe asked his brother.

"Yes, I'm talking to you," the old man called. "I am if that's your van parked back at B and J's Garage. Well, ain't it?"

"Yes, it is," Frank answered.

"Well, you'd better git on back there pronto," the old man called, waving his arms, "because your van's on fire! And it's a-burning like dry tumbleweed!"

23

3 Cowboys and Hardys

Frank and Joe ran at top speed toward Bill Hunt's garage. Their van was parked at the side, so they couldn't see it until they rounded the corner. Then they stopped and just stared.

Their van—the van that used to be owned by the Bayport Police Department, the van they had spent weeks cleaning, painting, and putting special equipment into, to say nothing of the dynamite sound system—wasn't on fire at all. It was sitting there just as safe and sound as they had left it.

A moment later they heard laughter behind them that sounded more like a donkey trying to sing. It was the old man in the plaid shirt. His bushy beard shook as he laughed.

"Aaahhh—that was a good 'un!" he said between guffaws. "You fellers jumped in with both feet."

"Very funny," Joe said. But he wasn't smiling.

"Thanks. I thought so," said the old man. "I was just funning you a little bit. Can't an old man have a laugh? This is still a free country, ain't it?"

Frank had to smile at the old guy who said everything with earth-shaking emotion.

"It's still a free country," Frank said. "And Axeblade is definitely one of its more interesting places."

"You bet. Well, just to show you we're still pals," said the old man, "I'll buy you some grub at Becky's Café."

When he heard food mentioned, Joe's attitude toward the old man changed a thousand percent. "You mean there's another restaurant, and we can really get something to eat in this town?"

"It's not a restaurant. It's a café," the old man said. "That's different."

"I don't care what you call it, as long as they've got food," Joe said. "Do you think they'll actually serve us?"

"Mustard and potatoes! 'Course they'll serve you if you're with me. Don't you young whippersnappers know who I am?" said the old man, trying to stick out his thin chest proudly.

"The sun's so bright it's hard to tell," Frank said with a smile.

The old man took off his ten-gallon hat so Frank

and Joe could get a better look at him. "Axeblade Pete," he said. "They named this town after me. Or I was named after it. Been so long ago, I can't remember."

"Let's try to remember *after* breakfast," Joe said, his stomach growling.

"Sure thing," said Axeblade Pete.

As they walked away from the garage Bill Hunt approached them. He was just arriving to open up for the day.

"Still here?" he asked.

"We're making friends," Joe said, clapping a hand on Axeblade Pete's back.

Bill Hunt didn't say anything, but his eyes glared at the old man.

"Who knows? We might even get so popular here, one of us will have to run for mayor," Frank said with a laugh.

The trio turned away from Bill Hunt and strolled down the street to Becky's Café.

But just before they entered the café, Frank slowed down a step so he could say something quietly to Joe. "Don't turn around, but we're being followed," he said. "Jeans, blue workshirt, leather vest, mirrored aviator sunglasses."

Joe nodded and pushed open the door to the crowded, noisy café. The smell of hot breakfast made his stomach growl again.

"I'll show you which one is the best table," Axeblade Pete said, pulling his two guests across the sawdust-covered tile floor to a round wooden table near the front window. The table was covered with a red-and-white checkerboard tablecloth.

"This looks like every other table in the place," Joe said. "What makes it the best?"

Axeblade Pete tapped his forehead with his finger without saying anything.

A tall young man with tight jeans, a blue workshirt, and a leather vest came in and sat down at the table next to them. He was wearing mirrored sunglasses.

"Boys, here comes Miss Becky, so order up a storm, 'cause I'm treating," said Axeblade Pete.

Frank and Joe looked up at the woman coming their way. Becky was a pretty woman of about forty. Her blue eyes were large, and they seemed to make decisions about people quickly. Her blond hair was twisted up in back, but that didn't stop a few curls from falling into her face. She wiped her hands off on her apron, which was made of the same checkerboard material as the tablecloths.

"No way, Axeblade," Becky said to the old man. To Frank and Joe's surprise, her accent wasn't Western. She sounded like she had grown up in the East. Then she looked at Frank. "Did he tell you he was treating?"

Frank and Joe nodded.

"Now, just hold your horses, Miss Becky," Axeblade Pete sputtered.

"He tells that to everyone," Becky said, shaking her head. "But he doesn't have a dime. This'll be his third breakfast today. Get out of here, Axeblade, at least until lunch."

"All right." The old man grumbled, but he obeyed like a child, tipping his hat to the Hardys and hurrying out the door.

"I suppose you want *us* to leave, too?" Frank asked.

"What for?" asked Becky.

Frank and Joe stared at her silently for a minute. Was someone in this town finally being friendly?

"Don't you know who we are?" said Joe.

"I'm a café owner, not a mind reader," she said with a laugh. She stuck her hand out to shake. "Becky Waldo."

"Frank Hardy," Frank said. "And this is my brother, Joe."

"Now that we've had the introductions, let's discuss the menu. What do you say?" Joe said eagerly.

"Take your time," Becky told the Hardys, handing them menus. Then she looked over at the man in the sunglasses at the next table. "And what do you want, Sly Wilkins?"

"Coffee, Becky," he said in a rough voice.

"I'll come back for your orders, guys," Becky said to Frank and Joe. And with that, she walked away toward the kitchen.

A minute later, a twelve-year-old boy with dark straight hair and dark eyes brought two large glasses of fresh orange juice to Frank and Joe. He wore Western jeans, white high-topped leather sneakers, and black leather wristbands with silver studs.

"Hey, what's happening? Becky says you guys are hungry. My name's Kwo," the boy said in a friendly voice. "That's Vietnamese for how-do-I-get-out-of-this-town?" He laughed, took a deep breath, and went on talking quickly. "Becky's my mom. Not my real mom, my adopted mom. And Tom, her husband, he was my dad, but he's dead now. You're the two with the blue van down at Bill Hunt's garage, aren't you?"

Before Frank or Joe could answer, he went on, "You're from Bayport, back East—I saw the bumper sticker from your high school. I've never been there, but then that's no big deal. I've never been *anywhere* except Vietnam and Axeblade—and they wouldn't have been my first and second choices, I'll tell you. Hey, you guys have got enough camping supplies in your van to last you a month. I'll bet you're driving cross-country and camping out, aren't you?"

"Whew! You know everything, don't you, Kwo? I'll bet you're the guy to talk to when we need information," Frank said with a smile. "Yeah, we're camping out, all right. And we made the mistake of camping in the national park last night, but—"

"But you got beat up," Kwo said, finishing Frank's sentence. "I know. The whole town's talking about it."

"I wish someone would talk to us about it," Joe said.

29

"Yeah, well, don't take it personally," Kwo said. "People get real nervous around here when the trucks are running."

"Trucks? What trucks?" asked Joe.

"Tankers," Kwo answered.

"Those silver tanker trucks?" Joe said. "We saw them last night."

Frank and Joe could tell that Kwo had lots more to say. But just then the man with the mirrored sunglasses and leather vest—the man Becky had called Sly Wilkins—interrupted.

"Say, there, mighty mite, I thought your momma said she didn't like to see you standing in one place too long, especially at breakfast," he said.

"No big deal," Kwo said. But he took the hint and hurried away. Sly Wilkins propped his feet up on one of the chairs at his table.

Finally Becky came back with a large mug of hot coffee for Sly Wilkins and plates of French toast, sausages, home fries, and biscuits for Frank and Joe.

"But we didn't order anything," Joe said.

"Maybe I *am* a mind reader after all," Becky said, smiling. "Besides, this is what my cook does best. Need anything else?"

"Just a little information," Frank said, looking over at Sly Wilkins. "Kwo was telling us about those tanker trucks that came through last night. What were they hauling?"

Becky's eyes darted toward Sly once before she answered.

30

"Toxic wastes," she said. "Chemical wastes from some big factories near Dobbsville."

"Toxic wastes?" Joe said. "That stuff is dangerous. I can see why people get nervous when those trucks roll through town."

"It doesn't happen very often," Becky said. She tried to move away from their table.

"Every month, four nights in a row, to be exact," Kwo said as he walked by carrying a stack of dirty dishes. "Always after midnight. I know because sometimes I monitor the truckers on my CB."

"Where were they going last night?" Frank asked.

"Same place they always go. Ben Barntree's ranch," Kwo said. Becky shot him a scowling glance, and he scooted off to the kitchen.

"You mean they dump that poison on somebody's *ranch?*" Joe asked. He stopped eating, his forkful of potatoes hanging in mid-air.

"It's all legal," Becky explained, clearing the empty plates from a nearby table. "Ben Barntree has an enormous spread, the B-Bar-B Ranch, just this side of the park. He uses a small part of his land somewhere near the park for a dump."

"He uses land near the national park?" asked Frank. The memory of his being beaten up at the campsite in the park was still very fresh in his memory. "He doesn't like to chase people out

31

of the park when the trucks are coming, does he?"

Becky leaned her hands on Frank and Joe's table and lowered her voice. "You'd better be careful where you ask questions like that. Ben Barntree is on the town council and every kind of committee you can think of. He owns the most land, his bank holds mortgages on most of the property around here, and he's the richest, most powerful man in Axeblade. People around here have a special feeling about Ben Barntree."

"People around here have a lot of special feelings," Frank said. "But I don't understand most of them."

Becky smiled faintly and walked away.

"You know, you're doing more talking than eating. Your food's getting cold," Sly Wilkins said. He slid his feet off the chair he'd been using as a footstool and pushed his cowboy hat back on his forehead. "And that's kind of insulting to the cook."

"Good conversation helps you digest your food," Frank answered, staring right at the mirrored lenses of Sly's sunglasses.

"Fool idea like that must be why Easterners talk so much," Sly said loudly.

The noise of clattering dishes and casual conversation in the café almost stopped as the customers became more interested in Frank and Sly's conversation than in their own.

Sly pushed his chair back and stood up. "Now,

I could teach you a lesson or two about how to get along in the West," he said with a sneer.

"You couldn't teach us anything about tailing someone, because my brother spotted you following us all the way from Bill Hunt's garage," Joe said smugly.

If Joe's statement caught Sly Wilkins by surprise, he didn't show it. Frank and Joe watched him carefully.

"We like our foods spicy out here," Sly said. He picked up the glass pepper shaker on the table and slowly unscrewed the cap. Then he dumped all the pepper on Joe's French toast. "That'll put hair on your chest. Go ahead and eat it."

"Eat it?" Frank said angrily. "He can't even *find* it under all that pepper."

"I said eat it," Sly growled.

Joe's hands began to clench into fists, and Frank started to stand up. But before Frank could get to his feet, Sly kicked the chair out from under him. Frank fell flat on his back, hitting his head hard. The room began to spin, and the sounds of the café's customers laughing and whistling echoed as if they were coming from far away.

"That does it, you jerkface cowboy!" Joe shouted. He jumped up to grab Sly with one hand and give him an elbow chop with the other.

But just then Joe heard an old-fashioned Western rodeo whoop from somewhere behind him. And before he knew what was happening, a large

33

rope looped down over his head. It tightened around his chest with a jerk. He'd been lassoed from behind!

The next thing Joe knew, he was yanked to the floor with a smack—like a roped-and-tied steer!

34

4 Out of Town

Joe Hardy couldn't move his arms, but his legs were free. He twisted and kicked, trying to get off the floor. With every move, the rope around his chest tightened with a painful yank. Joe's struggle knocked over the table he and Frank had been sitting at. As the table tipped it spilled their breakfast all over Sly Wilkins.

"You little horsefly!" Sly shouted, moving toward Joe.

"Get 'em, Sly. Get 'em!" someone in the crowd shouted out.

Sly growled and lunged at both Hardy brothers on the floor. But Frank got to his feet to meet Wilkins. He tackled Sly around the middle, slamming him into a wall. Sly looked dazed for a minute, but he straightened himself up quickly. A kick of his black, pointed cowboy boot caught Frank in the shin. When Frank backed away in pain, he tripped over a toppled chair. The fall hurt twice as much because he landed on bruises from the beating the night before.

Suddenly there came the sound of metal banging.

"Stop it! Stop it right now!"

It was Becky, shouting from the kitchen and banging on a heavy black iron skillet with a wooden spoon. "The next person to move will get his head flat enough to lay in my skillet!"

All movement stopped. Then the onlookers moved aside for Becky to come through.

"Phoenix Dawson, let go of that rope," Becky ordered. "You want to show off your rope tricks, join a rodeo."

At last Joe felt the rope cutting into his arms loosen. He stood up and let the rope drop around his feet. Then he took a good look at the man who had lassoed him—the man Becky had called Phoenix Dawson.

Phoenix was a cowboy in his twenties with curly blond hair spilling out from under his cowboy hat. He wore the jeans, cowboy boots, and white T-shirt that seemed to be the uniform in Axeblade. Joe laughed when he noticed that Phoenix was wearing spurs, even though he was nowhere near a horse. He was really playing up the rodeo act for all it was worth, Joe decided.

"I was just trying to make it a fair fight," Phoenix said to Becky with a smile. "Both of them jumping on poor Sly—that wouldn't be right."

"Roping someone from behind isn't my idea of fighting fair," Becky snapped. Then she focused her anger on Sly Wilkins. She stood in front of him, turning the black iron skillet in her right hand. Sly stared at it as if he were looking down the barrel of a loaded shotgun.

"Becky, don't forget your New Year's resolution about losing your temper," Sly said. "I was just having a little fun."

The word "fun" really rubbed Joe the wrong way. "You've been breathing down our necks all day," he said to Sly. "You call that fun?"

"We have not," Phoenix Dawson said.

"Shut up, Phoenix," Sly growled.

Becky looked from Phoenix to Sly. But Frank and Joe looked at each other. "We"? Phoenix had said "we." Frank had spotted Sly trailing them. But it was news that *two* men were on their case. Who wanted them followed so closely it was a two-man job? Sheriff Arthur? Bill Hunt?

"You don't have brains enough to run out of a burning building," Sly said angrily to his young cowboy friend.

"I want to know what you guys are up to," Becky said to Phoenix and Sly.

But they didn't stay long enough to answer her. Immediately they headed for the door. Before he left, however, Sly turned around. He drew an

37

invisible gun from an invisible holster at his hip and shot Frank and Joe through the heart.

After the two cowboys left, the café customers went back to their food and ignored Frank and Joe.

Frank smiled and said to Becky, "Thanks for your help."

"Just clean up the mess and we'll consider the broken dishes paid for." Becky pointed to the overturned table, dishes, and spilled food. She walked away.

Joe pushed the mess together with his feet. "What's she mad at us about? They started that fight on purpose," he said.

"I know," Frank said. "I don't get it."

"Want to bet Sly and Phoenix were in the gang that jumped us in the park last night?" Joe asked.

Frank shrugged. Guessing—that's how his brother worked. But Frank was different. He just picked up pieces of broken plates, trying to fit them together. It was like a puzzle. And so was the mysterious, unfriendly town of Axeblade. "I was thinking about that line of Dad's," Frank said. " 'Remember what was going on just before a fight broke out. Sometimes people start a fight to change the subject.' "

Joe thought for a moment. "Becky was talking about toxic wastes being dumped on Ben Barntree's ranch," he said. "But she also said that everything was legal."

"I know," said Frank.

In his mind he was trying different pieces of the puzzle. He and Joe had been beaten and carried out of the park on the same night the tanker trucks went through to dump a load of waste on Ben Barntree's land. Coincidence? Or could it be a clue? Sly had started the fight just when Becky was telling them about the toxic dumping. Two coincidences? That made Frank suspicious.

And why were they beaten up in the first place? Did Barntree have anything to do with it?

"Maybe we should just take a look at Ben Barntree's ranch," Frank said as he and Joe carried the remains of their breakfast dishes through a swinging door into the kitchen.

They dumped the broken plates in a garbage can, and the cook, wearing a grease-spattered apron, looked up at them. Then the door swung open and Becky came in, reciting several late breakfast orders. She motioned Frank and Joe aside. "I've got to know something," she said. "Were they really following you, or was that just a story?"

"It's the truth," Joe said.

Becky looked at the Hardys with unblinking deep blue eyes, her head cocked slightly sideways. "Why?" she asked.

"That's what we'd like to know," Joe said.

"Something strange is going on in Axeblade. We don't know what yet. But we can feel it," Frank said, lowering his voice.

"Maybe you two ought to just stand in one

place till your van's fixed," Becky said with a nervous laugh.

"That's not what we do best." Frank smiled.

"We want to see Ben Barntree's ranch," Joe said. "Do you know of a car we could borrow to get out there?"

"Well, you can forget about borrowing mine," Becky said. "Everyone in town knows it, and I don't want people seeing *you* using *my* car to snoop on Ben Barntree."

"Why? Are you afraid of him?" asked Frank.

Becky scowled; she didn't like that question. She turned around and carried out a plate of scrambled eggs and ham steak to a customer.

But when Becky came back into the kitchen, she motioned Frank and Joe to follow her through the back door of the restaurant. She led them to a small garage in back. As they went in their footsteps kicked up sawdust in the sunlight.

In one corner of the garage a large object was covered with a white plastic sheet. Becky walked over and jerked the covering away.

When the dust settled, Frank and Joe were looking at an old, red Harley-Davidson motorcycle.

"This was my late husband's," Becky said. "If you can get it started, you can use it."

Joe was in heaven just looking at the classic motorcycle. He had always dreamed of having a Harley Sportster, but they were expensive and hard to find. But Frank was puzzled.

"I don't get it," he said to Becky. "Why are you helping us?"

"Let's just say I'm the kind of person who likes to do something first and figure out why later." Becky brushed her hair off her forehead and walked briskly back to the restaurant. But at the kitchen door she stopped. "That's not true. I know why I'm doing it," she said. "It's for Tom."

She came back to the bike, walking around it. Occasionally she rested her hand on the handlebars.

"See, my husband, Tom, died very mysteriously," she said. "He was having some kind of running battle with Ben Barntree. I don't know what it was about—he never told me. He joked and said it wasn't none of my concern, ma'am— he loved to imitate the way people talk out here. But whatever the trouble was, it bothered him. Sometimes he'd leave the café, hop on this bike, and ride, ride for hours. That's what he always did back home in Maryland, too. It was the only way he could work out problems."

She was quiet, smiling, but also sad.

"You said he died mysteriously?" Frank said.

"It's not a mystery if you ask the sheriff," Becky said. "To him it was just an accident. Tom was rock climbing in the national park, and they say he slipped and fell. They found his body at the base of the mountains. But I don't believe it was an accident, and it wasn't suicide."

"What was it?" asked Joe.

41

"In my heart of hearts, I think it was Barntree," Becky said coldly.

"Why?" said Joe.

Becky wiped away a tear. "Lots of reasons. The way Barntree acted around Tom, among other things. And the fact that a few years after Tom and I came to Axeblade, Myra Slack's husband died in an 'accident' like Tom's. If you ask Myra, she'll tell you Ben Barntree was responsible. But don't listen to me. I'm just a hysterical widow. That's what Ben Barntree said. And in the end, I couldn't prove a thing. So why don't you guys see if you can do something with this bike?"

"We will," Frank said. "We definitely will."

Becky left, and Frank and Joe got busy working on the motorcycle, trying to get it to start. Soon Kwo came into the garage. He walked around, kicking his feet through the sawdust.

"That's my dad's bike, you know," Kwo said.

Frank and Joe nodded. They could hear the jealousy in Kwo's voice.

"He wanted me to have it when I was old enough," Kwo said. "I've been taking care of it."

"You've done a great job," Joe said. "You took the battery out, drained the gas and oil, kept the bike clean and dry."

"Just like he taught me," Kwo said. He walked around the bike, looking over Frank and Joe's shoulders as they worked on the starter.

"If we get it started, you'll get the first ride," Frank said.

"Nobody could start that bike but my dad," Kwo said. "It's temperamental. He said you have to talk to it politely."

Joe sensed they weren't just shaking dust off an old bike to ride out to Ben Barntree's ranch. They were shaking dust off Kwo's memories. "Thanks. That's good to know." Joe smiled at Kwo.

Kwo left the garage for a while, but he kept coming back.

"I used to ride it all the time—even when I was little. I'd sit behind my dad and hold on to him as tight as I could." Kwo handed Joe a wrench. "Dad was funny. He said the bike had a mind of its own. I always said, no way—the carburetor just needs cleaning. He was probably right, though. I wish I'd told him he was right."

They talked some more about Kwo's adopted family and about Axeblade. Then later, when Kwo brought them lunch, he wanted to talk about Frank and Joe being detectives.

"How'd you hear about that?" Joe asked.

"I heard Bill Hunt talking to Mom," Kwo said.

Frank put down his sandwich. "We didn't need the publicity," he said seriously. "Now the whole town will know. If we're going to find out what's going on around here, we've got to start moving."

They sprang into high gear, but without a full set of tools, the work went slowly. It was almost dark before Frank and Joe had the motorcycle fixed up, gassed up, lubed, and ready to go. Joe Hardy straddled the bike and gave the kick-

43

starter everything he had. But the cycle responded with a sigh that sounded more like a laugh.

"I told you," Kwo said. "You have to be polite to it. Trust me."

Joe squinted one eye at Kwo. "That's my line," he said, laughing. "Okay, I'll give it a try." Slowly he patted the side of the bike. "Would you *please* start this time?" he said. Then he jumped on the kick-starter again. The cycle roared to life!

With Kwo behind him, Joe took the bike out for a test drive. They kept to back roads where no one would see them while Joe got used to the feel of the big cycle under him.

Then back at the garage Kwo hopped off. But Frank didn't hop on.

"It's too late," Frank said. "We can't see anything in the dark, and I sure don't want to try to spend another night in that park."

Joe agreed. So the Hardys spent the night sleeping on some blankets on the floor in the back of Becky's Café. In the morning they climbed on the motorcycle and rode out to Ben Barntree's B-Bar-B Ranch. The ranch began about eight miles west of town and stretched for hundreds of acres, right up to the edge of the national park.

"Do you want to try to find our campsite and see if our gear is still there?" Joe called to his brother.

"Not now," Frank answered. "Let's see what we can find out before Barntree gets rolling."

44

Just before they came to the park, Joe made a right onto a long road winding north through Barntree's land. A hot sun was rising in the eastern sky as they aimed north for the mountains in the distance.

"According to Kwo, the dump site is to the right. The park is to the left. And Barntree's ranch house is about halfway in between," Joe said.

"We'd better be quiet, if we're near Barntree's house," Frank said. He peered through the trees that lined each side of the road, looking for signs of life.

Joe downshifted to quiet the engine noise. Most of Barntree's land was treeless and flat, but the section nearest the park was wooded with pines. The land sloped very gently uphill.

Finally they came to a clearing and saw Barntree's long, stone ranch house set back about two hundred feet from his private road.

Joe immediately cut the cycle's engine, and they hopped off the bike, leaving it at the end of Barntree's dirt driveway.

They started to walk toward the house, not walking straight up the drive, but weaving in and out through the trees so they wouldn't be seen. A light, dry breeze brushed across the trees. It was the only sound they heard.

When they got close to the house, they also had a pretty good view of the pickup trucks and cars parked in the driveway. One van in particular caught Frank and Joe's attention. It was maroon, with an expensive, detailed airbrush painting on the side—a skeleton riding a beautiful galloping mustang horse with fiery eyes across a sky thick with clouds.

"Now that is a weird pizza-delivery truck," Frank joked. "Some rancher must have paid a fortune for that."

Joe was about to answer when he heard something that made every muscle in his body freeze. It started in the distance, but it was coming closer and closer very quickly.

"Guard dogs!" Joe said. "Lots of them!"

"Run for the bike!" Frank said. "Let's get out of here!"

They turned and ran down the driveway as fast as they could. Frank's heart raced, not from running but in response to the terrible, ferocious sound of the barking. It sounded like there were at least six dogs, and they were big—and fast!

Joe reached the bike first, leapt on it, and started jumping on the kick-starter. Once, twice, three times. "Please. *Please* start," Joe said, trying to be polite.

But no matter what he did, the bike wouldn't start. And the dogs were getting closer all the time!

5 A Watery Clue?

"Forget the bike!" Frank shouted as the pack of barking guard dogs tore across the yard, heading straight for them.

Joe hopped off the useless motorcycle and looked for a tree to climb. But none had branches sturdy enough near the bottom. The brothers began to get desperate. They knew they could never outrun the dogs—and besides, there was no place to go.

Worse yet, they were completely unarmed—and bare-armed, too. If the dogs attacked, they'd tear right into flesh. The Hardys' only hope of avoiding attack was to find shelter somewhere—a place where the dogs couldn't get at them.

"Let's try the cars!" Joe yelled.

47

Although it meant doubling back toward the house and toward the dogs, Frank followed Joe. They made a wide circle through the woods and ran as fast as they could to the nearest car parked in Barntree's driveway. It was a big yellow Cadillac convertible.

Joe yanked at the door handle on the driver's side. A look of panic filled his eyes. "Door's locked!" he shouted.

"They're coming!" Frank called back. His eyes were locked on a small pack of tan-and-black German shepherds twenty yards away. The dogs were rushing at them like a football team at kickoff, barking angrily.

Frank ran over to the maroon van with the airbrushed picture of the skeleton rider. He jerked the handle of the van's side door, and the door slid open. There was no time to be surprised or relieved. He just jumped in.

"Come on!" he shouted to his brother.

Then Frank saw what was happening to Joe. Joe was trying the doors of a jeep when the dogs got to him. But the jeep was locked! The leader of the pack almost tore into Joe's leg. Joe managed to jump on the jeep's hood just in time. He kicked at the dogs as they circled and jumped around the jeep, trying to reach him.

Frank knew that Joe couldn't hold the dogs off for long. He had to do something fast to keep his brother from being attacked.

"Hey!" Frank suddenly shouted. He jumped out of the maroon van, waving his arms and yelling. "Sit! Heel! Stay! Play dead, you dumb dogs!"

The dogs' heads jerked toward Frank. They changed directions so fast that their paws skidded, kicking up dirt.

As soon as the dogs left the jeep to charge Frank, Joe jumped off the hood.

"Get in the van!" Frank called.

Joe ran at top speed toward the rear of the van, whooping and calling to get the dogs' attention. Frank was only a few feet away, near the front. For an instant, the huge animals were confused. They slowed, not knowing which intruder to go for. That hesitation was just what Frank and Joe needed.

They both ran for the open side door of the maroon van, leapt in, and slammed the door just before the dogs got there. The six shepherds jumped, smashing against the side of the van, beating their heavy bodies against the metal. They ran around the truck, barking, jumping, scratching, digging at the glass, the doors, the sides.

"There goes that awesome paint job," Joe said.

"We'll think of an apology later," Frank said.

After a few minutes, the dogs gave up jumping on the van and started circling it, barking every time they saw Frank or Joe through the windows.

Inside, the Hardys checked out the van. It had thick carpeting and comfortable leather seats in front. The bench seat in back had been replaced by two saddles, side by side, mounted on metal posts that stuck up two feet from the floor of the van. There was a refrigerator and track lighting, and on the wall opposite the sliding door, a small, old-fashioned jukebox was hooked up to the van's stereo tape deck.

"I found some flares," Frank said, digging around in the back.

"Those mutts probably eat them for dog bis-cuits," Joe said. "Too bad this guy didn't leave his keys."

For a minute both Hardys continued to search. "This is what *our* van should look like," Joe said.

"Yeah," Frank agreed, climbing into one of the saddles.

"So what do you think? Is this Barntree's?" Joe asked.

"I don't know. I don't see a name on anything," Frank said. "But somebody put some bucks into fixing this thing up. Barntree is as good a guess as any."

"You know what I'd like to find here?" Joe's face was grim. "A ski mask. Something to connect Barntree with those guys who attacked us night before last."

"It's worth a look," Frank said, climbing out of the saddle. "It's pretty quiet outside. Did the dogs give up?"

Joe looked out the window. The dogs were still outside, playing a waiting game. When they saw Joe, they jumped to their feet, barking and snap-ping.

"No, they're sitting there, waiting patiently

for their dinner," Joe said. "Why hasn't anyone come out to find out what the dogs are barking about?"

"In Axeblade, probably everyone's dog is a killer," Frank said. "People are used to it."

Joe opened the glove compartment and looked through the papers inside, but there was no ski mask—only maps and a pair of leather gloves.

Then he noticed a yellow pad on the front passenger's seat. He picked it up, and immediately something slipped out from between the pages onto the floor. It was a letter and an envelope.

"Looks like we were wrong about this being Barntree's van," Joe said, picking up the envelope and handing it to Frank.

The empty envelope was addressed to Robbie McCoy, Skeleton Rider Ranch, Axeblade. The return address was that of a civil engineering firm in Lawton.

Joe read the letter aloud:

"Dear Mr. McCoy,
    "After careful consideration of your plan to divert water from the Canary River in Lawton to your cattle ranch in Axeblade, I must advise against it. From an engineering standpoint, it would be a very expensive proposition."

The letter had been signed by one of the engineers of the firm.

"I don't get it," Joe said. "Why does this guy

51

need water all the way from Lawton? There must be plenty of water around here."

"Maybe not on his land, or maybe Axeblade's drying up." Frank eased again into one of the saddles in back. "That was written yesterday."

"I'll bet this is hot news, and Robbie McCoy is in there talking to Barntree about it," Joe said, putting the letter back into the pad of paper.

"Could be," Frank said. He leaned forward and glanced out the van window to be sure no one was coming. His eyes darted to the other windows. "That's strange."

"What is?" Joe asked. "What do you hear?"

"Nothing," Frank said with concern. "Why are the dogs so quiet?"

Joe leaned toward the front and looked out the passenger-side door. Then he twisted to look out the driver's door. "They're quiet because they've gone," he said.

There was something very strange about a pack of carefully trained killer dogs just disappearing all by themselves. Had someone called them off? And if so, why? Did Barntree know that Frank and Joe were in the van? They didn't have time to figure it out. They just wanted to get off Barntree's property while the getting was good.

"Let's go," Joe said.

They went to the van's sliding door, ready to run for their lives.

But before Joe could reach for the handle, the door flew open—and someone stuck a double-barreled shotgun right in Joe's face!

6 Questions—But No Answers

Frank and Joe didn't speak, didn't breathe. They just stared at the barrel of the shotgun, which moved when they moved. It followed them like a cobra about to strike its prey.

"You know these two, Robbie?" asked the man holding the shotgun. Robbie, a much younger man, came forward from a few feet behind.

"No. I don't know who they are, Ben," Robbie said stiffly. "Do you?"

Now the Hardys knew whom they were facing. The man with the gun had to be Ben Barntree. He was in his fifties, with skin that had been dried and tanned from years of working in the sun. His blue jeans were baggy, and they drooped below his protruding belly.

53

The younger man, who looked to be in his late twenties, had red hair. A wide-brimmed cowboy hat shaded his fair, freckled face. Joe immediately guessed that this was Robbie McCoy, the van's owner. The same Robbie McCoy the letter had been sent to.

"Look what they did to my van!" Robbie suddenly yelled as he noticed the scratches made by the jumping dogs. He pounded on the side of his van. "The paint job's ruined! You know what that cost me?"

"We didn't do that. Those dogs did it," Joe said.

"I'm going to kill you jokers," Robbie said, glaring at Frank and Joe. But Ben Barntree very calmly reached out and put a firm hand on Robbie's arm. It was like a clamp, holding him from doing anything more.

"Relax, Robbie," Ben Barntree said quietly, finally letting go of Robbie's arm. "I'll pay for the paint job. And it'll be good as new. You've got my word on it."

Robbie whirled on his heels and walked away. He stood with his back to the van, looking off into the distance. But he didn't say anything more. It was as if Barntree's quiet promise had really been an order Robbie didn't dare refuse—an order to shut up and stop making waves.

Frank and Joe began to sense the power of Ben Barntree. It wasn't in his looks. It wasn't in the tone of his voice, which was deep and very smooth. It was in the confidence he had about what he could make happen. His easy, quiet manner was just his way of saying, "Don't you dare cross me because you know what I'll do if you do."

Barntree turned back to the Hardys. "What are you two doing here?" he asked. "You're not supposed to be in that truck or on my land."

"We got lost," Frank lied. "We thought we were on a public road."

"Then all of a sudden it was dog city everywhere we looked," Joe added. "We jumped in the van to get away from them."

"Well, boys, this isn't a public road. You're on the B-Bar-B Ranch. And my wife doesn't feel safe without those dogs," Barntree explained calmly. "That's why I have 'em."

"Sorry about your van," Frank said to Robbie. Robbie stared at Frank without answering, but his face seemed to soften a little.

"What are you fellas doing on that motorcycle, anyway?" Barntree asked. "I thought your van was being fixed."

Is there anyone in Axeblade who doesn't know about Joe and me? Frank wondered to himself.

"And isn't that Tom Waldo's old bike?" asked Ben Barntree, rubbing his chin.

"Becky let us use it to see the sights," Frank said.

"Did she?" Barntree said. He said it like a question and like a comment to himself. "Fellas, those dogs don't like to be fenced in for too long. I think you'd better be going."

55

"Can't. The bike's dead," Joe said. "It won't start."

"Robbie, why don't you haul the boys back to town?" Barntree said. "I'll take care of getting the bike back to Becky."

"No way, Ben," Robbie said. "Why should I help them out? They ruined my van!"

"Robbie, I'm asking you," Ben Barntree said in a low, gentle tone of voice.

He was doing it again—using that quiet tone of voice to let everyone know that he meant business. And the message came across loud and clear: Barntree was saying, "If you want me to stay as calm as I am now, do what you're told."

Robbie turned and walked around to the driver's door of his van.

"And, fellas," Ben Barntree said casually to Frank and Joe before they drove away, "be careful you don't get lost anymore."

Frank and Joe knew a threat when they heard one.

Robbie started the engine, drove down Barntree's road, and then headed for Axeblade. He drove fast, the way everyone drove on the flat Western highways. He didn't say anything on his own as he drove, so Frank and Joe tried to get some information out of him—at first by sounding like tourists instead of detectives.

"Barntree's got a big ranch," Frank said, sitting in the passenger seat of the van, watching Wyoming fly by his window.

56

"Yeah," Robbie said, his eyes unblinking and focused on the road.

"You work for him?" Frank asked, as if he hadn't secretly read the letter addressed to Robbie at the Skeleton Rider.

Robbie looked at Frank out of the corner of his eye. "Huh-uh," he said. "Got my own ranch."

"You must have really saved your allowance," Joe said loudly from a saddle seat in back.

"The Skeleton Rider was my dad's ranch—my granddad's and great-granddad's before that."

Okay, Frank thought. So much for getting to know you. Let's start digging a little. Maybe Robbie knows something about Barntree. Or about what Barntree might be trying to hide. He looked back at Joe and then turned to look out the window, away from Robbie.

Joe Hardy got the signal—his brother was telling him to watch Robbie McCoy's face.

"I hear Barntree's got a toxic dump," Frank said casually. Robbie's face didn't move, except for a little twitching squint Joe caught.

"You guys are slow learners," Robbie said. "You should stay out of other people's business."

"We just wondered where he's dumping the stuff," Frank said. "Because toxic chemicals usually kill off vegetation. But the trees and bushes seem to be growing just fine around Barntree's house."

Robbie suddenly hit the brakes, leaving a strip of black tire rubber three car lengths long.

"Don't wonder about it," Robbie said. He reached back, slamming open the van's sliding door. The free ride was over—even though they hadn't quite reached town.

Frank and Joe hopped out of the van and got their first good look at the damage the dogs had done. The beautiful Skeleton Rider painting was ruined. Deep scratches cut across the clouds, the skeleton, and the sky. In fact, the whole van would have to be repainted. It made Joe feel bad when he saw it.

"What do you think of him?" Joe asked his brother as they walked the remaining two miles back to town.

"Robbie? I don't know," Frank said. "But his jeans are torn at the bottom—just like one of those five guys who jumped us two nights ago."

"Yeah. I saw that, too," Joe said.

When the Hardys reached Axeblade, the first thing they did was explain to Becky about the motorcycle. She shook her head, saying, "I never learn," but she didn't look too angry. Then they went to Bill Hunt's garage to see if their van had been fixed.

Heavy-metal music was blasting out of Bill Hunt's tape player. When he saw the Hardys, he turned it off.

"What's the story on our van?" Frank asked.

"I got the fan belt on, but I'm still waiting for a water pump," said the mechanic. "You guys in a hurry now?"

Frank and Joe nodded their heads.

Bill's face lit up. "Leaving Axeblade?" he asked enthusiastically.

"Nope," Joe answered. "We just want to have our own wheels back so we can get around."

Bill Hunt gave a short, sarcastic laugh, going back to work on the engine of his pickup.

"You guys are a fight looking for a place to happen," he said over his shoulder.

"I thought it already had happened," Frank answered. "Twice. First in the park two nights ago, and then yesterday morning in Becky's Café."

"What happened yesterday?" Bill looked surprised.

"Nothing much. Two guys—one named Sly Wilkins and the other named Phoenix Dawson— tried to give us a hard time," Frank said. "They were playing git-along-little-dogie, and we were the little dogies, that's all."

"I'm surprised you haven't heard about it," Joe said. "I thought Main Street was a regular telegraph line, the way news travels up and down it."

Bill got a strange, distant look on his face, as though he was making up his mind about something. Then he turned without saying anything and wrote in the dirt on the pickup truck's door, "Check the fence."

Frank stared at the message for a moment in silence. He was about to ask Bill what it meant when he heard footsteps behind him.

"Hi, Billy," said a sweet voice.

As soon as the woman spoke, Bill erased the

words on the truck with his hand. Frank and Joe looked to see who was standing behind them.

She was young, about twenty-two years old. She wore a short denim skirt, pink tennis shoes, and a pink tank top. When she stepped farther into the garage, Frank and Joe couldn't miss the fact that she also smelled of floral soap.

"Hi, Sara," Bill Hunt said uncomfortably.

Nobody said anything after that for a moment.

"I'm Bill's sister, Sara," the woman said to Frank and Joe. "We'd probably be old and gray before my little brother has manners enough to introduce us."

Bill Hunt suddenly seemed nervous. "What's up, Sara?"

"Billy, what would you say about making me a small loan?" she said. She didn't seem embarrassed about asking in front of strangers.

"I'd say why don't you ask your husband," her brother answered.

"Because there's no use throwing your bucket down a dry well," Sara said with a giggle.

Bill Hunt walked away, toward his office.

"Well, gee," she said. "I heard about what happened in the park to you guys the other night. I'm real sorry."

"It wasn't your fault," Joe said with a smile.

"You're from the East, right?" Sara said. "The farthest east I've been is to Atlantic City."

"It gets pretty wet if you go any farther east," joked Frank.

60

"What? Oh, you mean the Atlantic Ocean?" Sara said. Her laugh was open and lighthearted.

For a moment the Hardys almost forgot that they were in Axeblade, home of the deadly stare.

"Hey, how would you guys like a Western home-cooked meal tonight? Do you have any plans?"

"Sounds great to me," Joe said quickly.

Frank smiled, knowing that Joe was sick and tired of restaurant food.

Bill Hunt came back with some ten-dollar bills in his hand. He handed them to his sister.

"Thanks, Billy," she said. "I'd kiss you, but I can't find a spot on your face that isn't greasy." She put the money in the small straw purse that hung from her shoulder. "I've just invited Frank and Joe to dinner tonight," she said. "You're invited, too."

"No, thanks," said the mechanic.

"Don't you like my cooking?"

"You know why I don't want to come."

Brother and sister looked at each other for a moment. Frank and Joe could see that there was something each wanted to say to the other. And from the frown on Bill's face, what he wanted to say was obviously something that Sara wouldn't agree with.

Sara took out paper and pen from her purse and began to write. "This is our address," she told the brothers. "You'll find it easy. It's just a few blocks from Main Street. Come at six."

61

"Thanks," Frank said.

Then as soon as Sara had left, Joe asked, "What did you mean about check the fence?"

Bill Hunt looked around the garage nervously, as if someone might be listening. "I never said that," he said. Then he turned on the tape player and leaned into the engine of the pickup.

Joe and Frank walked out into the street and stood there for a minute, deciding where to go.

"We're finding more pieces to this puzzle all the time," Frank said thoughtfully. He was thinking about everything they had learned about Axeblade and the people who lived there. "Too bad we can't fit them together."

"I say we ask Kwo," Joe said. "He seems to be the gossip guru around here."

"Good idea," Frank said.

They immediately headed for Becky's Café, eager to get out of the hot afternoon sun. But a moment later they heard a familiar voice behind them, calling their names.

"Hardy boys! Hardy-Hardy-Hardy boys!"

They turned around and saw Axeblade Pete standing by the garage, his beard bouncing as he jumped up and down and waved his arms.

"What's up, Axeblade?" Frank asked.

"Your van's on fire!" the old man yelled.

"You already tried that one," Frank said.

But Axeblade Pete was going wild. He was jumping and yelling, "Have you two got sugar lumps for brains? I said your van's on fire!"

Frank slowly walked back to the garage, rounding the corner to look at their van.

Flames and smoke were coming out of the driver's-side window!

"Oh, no!" Frank shouted to Joe. "It really *is* on fire!"

7 Hot Times in the Old Town

Frank and Joe both raced to the burning van. More smoke than fire billowed from the windows—a good sign. Maybe they could put it out before the flames reached the gas tank. If they didn't, the whole thing was going to explode!

"It's a-burnin'!" Axeblade Pete shouted.

Frank ran into the garage, looking everywhere for Bill Hunt. "Where's a fire extinguisher?" Frank shouted. "Our van's on fire!"

Bill Hunt was in his office, talking on the telephone. At first he had a look of surprise on his face. Then he dropped the phone and grabbed a small, lightweight fire extinguisher off the wall of his office. He tossed it to Frank and carried a larger one out of the garage himself.

When they got to the van, Joe was doing what he could to put the fire out. He had the driver's door open, and he was beating at the flames with a blanket from the back of the van.

"It's a-burnin'!" Axeblade shouted again.

Frank wanted to strangle the old man but directed his energy toward the task at hand. Soon the fire extinguishers had smothered the fire. But they had also left a thick blanket of cold foam over everything. The van was a mess.

Bill Hunt dropped the large fire extinguisher on its side and sat on it as though it were a log. He wiped his sweaty face.

Frank and Joe looked inside the blue van. The thick smell of smoke stung their noses.

How had it happened? The detective in Frank had to find out. He stared at the driver's seat, which was burned the worst. The dashboard and window on the driver's side were scorched more than on the passenger side. Someone must have walked by and tossed a lit rag, maybe soaked in gasoline, onto the seat. No way had the fire started by accident. Someone had set it.

Frank noticed Joe's gloomy face and bumped his younger brother with his shoulder.

"Chill out," Frank said. "It's not so bad. Needs a good scrubbing down and towels on the seats for seat covers, that's all. And a water pump," he added, joking. "Lucky we got here in time."

"We've worked on this van for a year, and we've planned this trip for months!" Joe said loudly. "I'd like to line up everyone in this town and punch them all out." He turned to the person he wanted to start with, Bill Hunt. After all, who else had been so close? Who else could have set the fire so easily right after they left?

"What are you looking at me for?" asked Bill.

"You're supposed to be *fixing* our van. Well, it's fixed, all right," Joe said.

"Huh-uh. I didn't do this, guys," the mechanic told them. "But if it'll make you feel better, I'll keep it inside the garage from now on. And I'll leave the garage key over there"—he pointed to some scrap tires stacked outside the garage—"in case you need anything when I'm not around."

The offer didn't make Joe feel better. He slammed the van door and walked away.

Frank caught up with him. "Come on, Joe. Cool down. Start thinking like a detective again," he said. "It could have been anyone."

"For instance?"

"For instance, who told us about the fire?" asked Frank.

"Axeblade Pete," Joe said. He glanced at Frank. "You think it's the old I-can't-be-the-guilty-guy-because-I-tipped-you-off trick?"

"The old man was here. He could have set the fire. And at the very least he might have seen who did it," Frank said.

But when they looked up and down the street, Frank and Joe found that Axeblade Pete had disappeared from the scene. So they went looking for him at the most logical place they could think of—Becky's Café. He was there, standing

66

at the door, inviting people to have lunch with him—as long as they could pay.

"Hello, you young whippersnappers," Axeblade Pete said with a quick jerk of his head. "Some excitement this morning. It was a-burnin'!"

"That's what we want to talk to you about," Frank said.

"Sure. But let's do our palavering over some grub," said the old cowboy. "Spicy food—that's the secret of living a hundred and fifty years. And I should know—I'll be a hundred and twenty next month. You boys want to join me?"

Frank and Joe nodded. They weren't the least bit interested in spicy food, and they were pretty sure that Axeblade had overestimated his age by at least forty years. But they hoped that in between his tall tales and out-and-out lies they might hear something useful.

So once again they followed Axeblade to his favorite table in Becky's Café, where he sat down, unfolded a napkin, and tucked it under his chin.

"I tell you, boys, when I cut my finger, you know what comes out? Chili sauce," said Axeblade Pete. "It's the truth."

"Tell us something else that's true," said Frank. "What were you doing by the garage when our van was set on fire?"

"Boys, I'm not the kind of hombre that lets the grass grow under his feet. I'm a traveling man, that's for sure."

"While you were traveling past our van, did you see anyone messing with it?" Joe asked.

"Well," said Axeblade, looping his thumbs in the shoulder straps of his overalls, "I can't say that I did. And I can't say that I didn't."

"Huh?" Joe said.

"Boys, folks around here say old Axeblade Pete sees things nobody else sees. Only trouble is, they don't believe I see 'em when I see 'em."

"We'll take a chance. Tell us what you saw." Frank leaned closer across the table to the old man. "We'll believe you."

"Well, it's hard to say," said Axeblade Pete. "Hard to say on an empty stomach, that is." He suddenly called out, "Miss Becky, I'm abundantly hungry for a bowl of your chili."

Becky walked over to the table. "What are you going to pay for it with, Axeblade?" she asked. "And please don't tell me your good looks."

"It's on us," Frank said.

"Make that two bowls of chili," Axeblade Pete added quickly.

"But first you tell us who you saw by our van," Joe said.

"I heard about your fire," Becky told them.

"It was deliberately set," Joe said.

"I believe it." Becky lowered her voice. "But I'll bet the fire chief will tell you it was spontaneous combustion. That's his reason for every fire he can't explain—like the three fires I had in the café right after my husband died. Did it damage your van much?"

"It burned all the road maps showing us the way out of here," Joe said grimly. "So we're staying till we find out what's going on."

"You've got my vote," Becky said. "Tell them what you saw, Axeblade."

Axeblade Pete shrugged. "I saw a cowboy."

"Great. What did he look like?" Frank asked.

Axeblade Pete's lower lip went in and out nervously. "Well, at that exact minute, I happened to spot a dollar bill on the ground." The old man pulled a dollar out of the front pocket of his overalls, displaying it as if he were a magician about to do a trick. Then he put it away. "Well, when I was through picking up the money, the cowboy was gone. All I saw was his boots. They had real gold on their heels."

A clue! Frank quickly looked at Becky. "Sound familiar?" he asked.

"No one I know," she said. "I don't think I've ever seen gold-heeled boots in my life. Could be something Axeblade saw in a movie a hundred years ago."

"Do I still get my chili?" asked Axeblade.

Frank nodded.

"And lots of those little round crackers, too, if you please, Miss Becky," said Axeblade.

"You guys want something to eat?" Becky asked. She sounded genuinely sorry for the trouble they were having.

"Not just yet, thanks," Frank said.

Becky walked back toward the kitchen for Axeblade Pete's chili, stopping at tables along the way to pick up dirty plates or take an order.

In a couple of minutes, Kwo came out of the kitchen with two bowls of chili and a small mountain of oyster crackers. He put the bowls down in front of Axeblade Pete. The old man began to eat noisily.

"How's your case going?" Kwo said. "Ever since you told me yesterday about you two being detectives, I've been getting into this undercover detective stuff. I even went to the library and got out as many detective books as I could carry. Maybe I could help you."

"Okay, let's see what kind of detective you are. What do you make of this clue?" Frank asked. "What if you found a letter from someone in Lawton telling Robbie McCoy that it won't work to divert water from the Canary River to his land?"

Kwo's face drooped. "That's totally crazy."

"Why?" asked Frank.

"For one thing," said Kwo, "the Ruby River runs through Robbie's ranch. He's already got plenty of water for his cattle. Lots of ranchers around here use the Ruby."

Axeblade interrupted the slurping and gobbling noises he'd been making with a loud, disgusted snort through his nose.

"It just doesn't make sense for him to get water from somewhere else," Kwo said.

"If that don't make sense," Axeblade cut in, "then two and two don't add up to four."

"What are you talking about?" Joe asked.

"I'm saying that I wouldn't want any steer of mine drinking out of the Ruby River."

"Why not, Axeblade?" asked Frank.

"Because the Ruby ain't fit to drink with all that pollution." Chili dripped off his spoon and stuck in the old man's bushy beard.

Frank and Joe looked from Axeblade to Kwo. The young boy rolled his eyes and shook his head.

"It's all that poison they're burying on Ben Barntree's land that's doing it," said Axeblade. "Think they can hide it just by putting it in the ground." The old man pounded the table with his fist. "You can't hide from nature. It's got eyes everywhere."

Frank leaned back in his chair. He felt like he needed a scorecard to tell when the old man was crazy and when he was making sense.

"Right, Axeblade," Kwo said. "Anything you say." He leaned toward Frank and Joe. "Here's the story. The Ruby River is twenty miles away from the toxic dump on the B-Bar-B Ranch."

Then Axeblade leaned forward as if he were a part of the secret, too. His beard drooped into one of his empty bowls of chili. "Yeah, but listen to Axeblade Pete, boys," he said. "The Ruby is fed by a deep, underground spring that runs right smack through Ben Barntree's property."

No one said anything for a moment while the old man's spicy breath blew across at them.

"If the Ruby River is polluted, that would

71

explain why Robbie McCoy wants to divert fresh water onto his land," Joe said.

"Hold on, Axeblade," Kwo said, with a smile beginning to form at the corners of his mouth. "If the Ruby River is polluted by the spring on Barntree's property, then there'd be hundreds of sick cattle. But I haven't heard one person in town talk about losing a single head."

"It looked like McCoy and Barntree were good friends, too," Frank said. "McCoy wouldn't like the man who's polluting his river and killing his cattle."

The old man didn't answer. "When I was a little boy, I got lost in the woods," he said. "A wolf and an eagle fought over who'd be my mama. I *know* things. Nature talks to me. Animals talk to me. Sometimes the clouds send me letters." He stood up and walked out of Becky's Café.

Becky passed the table again. "Where'd Axeblade go?" she asked.

"He just got up and left. I think we hurt his feelings," Frank said.

"Usually when he does that, he doesn't want to answer a question," Becky assured them.

"But what he said made so much sense—for a while," Joe said. "Do you know if the Ruby River is fed by a spring on Barntree's land?"

Becky shrugged.

"I guess there's only one way to find out," Frank said.

72

"A late-night trip to Barntree's ranch?" Joe asked.

Frank nodded. "We'll watch the tank trucks—and this time, no one will chase us away."

"Sounds good. You guys want something to eat now?" Becky asked.

"Sure," Frank said. "But don't count on us for dinner. We've been invited out."

"Well, excuse me, now you're the Popularity Brothers," Becky joked. "Seriously, which of the friendly people of Axeblade invited you?"

"Bill Hunt's sister," Joe said. "We met her at the garage. Besides you and Kwo, she's the first friendly person we've met here."

Becky's mouth twitched with surprise. "You've got to be joking," she said.

"No, we're not," Joe said. "Why? What's wrong with Sara inviting us to dinner?" he asked.

"Sara Hunt is married to Phoenix Dawson, that's all," Becky said.

Frank and Joe stared at each other in surprise. Phoenix Dawson was the cowboy who'd lassoed Joe during their fight with Sly Wilkins in Becky's Café the day before. So why was Dawson's wife being so nice to them?

It didn't make sense, but there was only one way to find out. Go to dinner at Sara Dawson's house—and keep their guard up.

To kill time, Frank and Joe helped Becky clean up the café after the lunch crowd. When it was nearly six, the Hardys stepped outside into the cool evening breeze. There was something strange in the air—something odd about the empty streets. They walked quietly to the address Sara had given them, 123 Pine Barren Lane.

They found the tiny yellow house easily. A picket fence bordered the small square of land. Frank opened the gate, and they walked in slowly, looking around to see if they were being watched.

"Something weird's going on," both Hardys said at the same time.

"The mailbox," Frank said. "It doesn't say Dawson *or* Hunt. It says Morningside. What were you going to say?"

"If Sara's expecting us, why aren't there more lights on in the house?" Joe said. "It almost looks like no one's home."

Stepping onto the porch, they found a note on the door: F & J. Doorbell doesn't work. Come on in.

Frank and Joe stood for a long moment, not moving.

"I don't smell dinner cooking," Joe said. "I smell a trap. We're being set up."

Frank agreed. But just to be sure, they went around to the side and back of the house and looked in the windows. No one was home.

"Let's go," Joe said nervously.

They walked out the gate and went back up Main Street. What could they do until dark? They had a lot of time to kill before the trucks would be bringing the poisonous chemicals to dump on Ben Barntree's land.

The growl in Joe's stomach told them they'd better do something about dinner first. They went back to the garage. Bill Hunt wasn't around, but he'd left the key under the scrap tires as he'd promised. Joe and Frank dug around in the back of their scorched van and pulled out some peanut-butter crackers, a hunk of salami, a box of cookies, and three containers of juice.

After dinner they used the garage pay phone to call their parents, just to check in with them. But there was no answer. Then Frank remembered that their parents had been planning to go away for a few days.

Still killing time, Joe and Frank wandered down Main Street. All of a sudden Joe saw the perfect diversion. Video games! He led his brother into an empty coin-operated launderette. Joe had total radar when it came to finding an arcade—even when it was only two small games in a laundry.

"One of my favorites—Flyswatter!" Joe cashed a dollar for quarters at the change machine.

They played a couple of games as the empty washing machines on one side of the laundry and the empty dryers on the other side stood like sentries at attention.

But during the fourth game, Sheriff J. P. Arthur came into the laundry. "Okay, boys, the game's over," he said. Frank looked up, surprised. Nothing about the sheriff matched. His friendly voice, his angry eyes, his wrinkled uniform, his clean cowboy boots. "Hands on the wall and spread your legs."

"Don't tell me there's a law against scoring too many points in this game," Joe said.

"We can do this the easy way or the hard way, whichever you want." The sheriff took his .38 out of the holster at his waist.

"What's going on?" Frank said.

"You're under arrest," said Sheriff Arthur. "For robbery!"

8 Behind Bars

"Robbery! That's the craziest thing I've ever heard!" Joe said.

The handcuffs closed tightly with a series of sharp metallic clicks. Frank and Joe stood with their arms pinned stiffly behind their backs. Two deputies shoved them around a lot during the frisking and handcuffing.

"You're in enough trouble, son. Calling me crazy just isn't going to help your cause," said the sheriff. He wiped his wet forehead with a handkerchief. Then he gave orders to his men. "Stuff 'em in a squad car, boys, and smile so the people looking on out there know we're proud to be doing our job."

"You're doing a number on us, Sheriff, but you're not doing your job," Frank said.

77

A few minutes later, Frank and Joe were standing in the small police station. The handcuffs were removed, and the sheriff ordered the brothers to empty their pockets and have their fingerprints taken.

"I knew you boys were trouble the first night I saw you," said the sheriff.

A deputy inked up the fingers on Joe's right hand. Then he stamped Joe's fingerprints, one by one, on a form. Afterward, he said with a laugh, "Hey, J.P., how about this?" The deputy grabbed Joe's hand and rubbed the ink off on Joe's shirt.

Sheriff Arthur and the two deputies burst out laughing.

Maybe it was the laughter, or the way the man who was supposed to be in charge laughed just as hard as the other two, that filled Frank with so much anger. "Sheriff," Frank said as he was being fingerprinted, "who are we supposed to have robbed? You'd better have some proof."

The sheriff smiled and showed his teeth. "I got more than proof. How long did it take you to notice that Olive Morningside was gone for the week?" J. P. Arthur asked.

"We don't know her," Joe said.

"She's an old widow and a Sunday school teacher," the sheriff said.

Morningside? That time the name clicked for Frank. It was the name on the mailbox at the address Sara Dawson had given them.

The sheriff cleaned his top teeth by running his

78

tongue over them. "You don't have to know her. But I got eyewitnesses, son, neighbors who say they saw you tonight at One Twenty-three Pine Barren Lane. You were there, weren't you?"

"We were there—because Sara Dawson told us to come there for dinner," Frank said.

"Yeah, she even wrote it down," Joe said. "What did you do with the stuff from our pockets?"

The sheriff opened a desk drawer and took out a plastic bag with a zip-lock top. He dumped the contents out on the desktop.

Joe looked through them. Then he shuffled the objects with his hands. "Hey, it's gone," he said. "What happened to that slip of paper?"

"Son, you got bigger things to worry about than a piece of paper that don't exist," said the sheriff. He shoved the Hardys' personal effects back into the bag and put it away. He pulled open another desk drawer and took out something that was rolled up in a piece of cloth. He dropped it on his desktop with a clunk.

The deputies pushed Frank and Joe up to the sheriff's desk so they could get a good look as Sheriff Arthur unrolled the cloth. Inside was shiny silver antique flatware—spoons, knives, forks.

"You boys want to tell me about this?"

"It's silverware," Joe said. "You eat with it when you have good table manners."

"You're starting to get on my nerves, son," said J. P. Arthur.

"We've never seen that before," Frank said.

"Yeah, *before tonight,* you mean, when you stole it," said the sheriff.

"I said we've never seen it before," Frank said. "We didn't steal anything."

"Son, earlier tonight I got an anonymous phone call that told me to check out your van. I did, because that's my job. And that's exactly where we found this silverware."

"Maybe so, but we didn't put it there," Frank said.

"It's a frame-up," Joe said.

"That's what they all say"—the sheriff sighed —"for a while." He leaned back in his chair, put his feet on the desk, and crossed his legs. It gave the Hardys a good look at the barely worn soles of his new boots. It also gave them a good look at the heels—which were gold-plated in back!

Suddenly Frank and Joe realized that their arrest wasn't a mistake that could be cleared up. It didn't matter what they said to the sheriff. He was working for someone who wanted them out of the way. He had set their van on fire, and now he was going to lock them up. They were in big trouble.

"Throw 'em in a cell," the sheriff ordered.

The two deputies began pushing and shoving again. But Frank planted his feet and wouldn't move. "A phone call. Aren't we allowed one phone call?" he said.

"What for?" asked the sheriff. "You don't have

any friends in this town. Oh, go on and make your one phone call."

Frank and Joe looked at each other.

"Mom and Dad are gone for the weekend," Joe said. Then he lowered his voice so only Frank could hear. "How about calling the police in Lawton?"

"They're not going to take our word for anything over the word of a neighboring sheriff," Frank answered. "No one would." Then he turned back to the sheriff. "What's the phone number for Becky's Café?"

The sheriff squinted his disapproval at them and wiped his forehead with his handkerchief again. "I wouldn't go dragging innocent people into this if I were you, son."

Frank wasn't interested in Sheriff Arthur's advice. He called Becky and asked her to come down to the police station as soon as she could.

For the next half hour, Joe paced the floor in the dark cell, and Frank sat on a mattress smelling of mildew. Finally Becky arrived, looking concerned and nervous. The deputy locked Becky in the cell and then walked away.

"What happened to you two?" Becky asked.

"We need your help," was all Frank said. "There's nobody else we can ask."

"I'll help you if I can," Becky said. "What can I do?"

"You've got to help us get out of here somehow," Frank said.

Becky looked at him for a moment. Frank knew, as her eyes covered his face, that she was looking for a sign, any sign, to show that he was kidding.

When she saw that Frank was serious, she scowled. "Help you break out of jail? It may look good in the movies," she said, "but it's against the law. Even if I *have* lived in this rotten town for eighteen years, I don't take to notions about the Wild West and taking the law into your own hands."

"Okay, I'm sorry," Frank said. "I told it to you too quickly. Let's calm down. The big picture is, we're being framed for a robbery we didn't do."

"J.P. says he has witnesses," she said.

"Sure, he has witnesses who saw us at One Twenty-three Pine Barren Lane," Joe explained. "That's where Sara Dawson told us to go. She even wrote the address down. But we knew something was fishy when we got there. Someone had left a note inviting us to walk right in. But the house looked empty, so we didn't go in. We left."

"Sara set us up, and someone hid the 'stolen' silver in our van," Joe said. "Sara's in on it, Phoenix has got to be in on it, and I'm sure the sheriff is in on it."

"J.P.?" Becky asked. "Now, just a minute, Frank. J. P. Arthur's got his faults, but I don't think there's anyone who's going to say he's a bad cop.'

"I'll say it," Joe said. "That address Sara Dawson wrote down for us has conveniently disappeared."

"Maybe it fell out of your pocket tonight," Becky said.

"But we're detectives, not robbers," Frank said.

"I know. Kwo told me. He thinks you two are the best thing to happen to this town since rainstorms during a drought," Becky said. "And that's another reason why you shouldn't break out of jail. It sets a bad example."

"We know breaking out of jail is wrong, but we don't have any choice," Frank said. "They're never going to let us go."

"If you're innocent—"

"*If* we're innocent?" Frank said, wiping his sweaty hands on his jeans.

"The idea in this country is to let a jury decide that," Becky said.

"But not in Axeblade. In Axeblade you've got a few people who act like sheriff, judge, and jury all rolled into one, and the rest of the people just sit there and take it," Frank said.

Becky winced as if someone had just stepped heavily on her foot.

"There's not going to be a trial," Frank went on. "They'll hold us for a while and then probably get us out of town somehow. Or maybe they'll have to get rough. There will be an accident. It all depends on whether they think we know too much. And the crazy thing is, we don't really know anything—yet."

83

"You're just trying to scare me with old memories," Becky said, her voice shaky.

"What if Barntree is one of them? Don't you still want to get him?" asked Joe.

Becky unpinned her long hair, pulled it tight and orderly, and pinned it back again. "Look, guys, after Tom died so mysteriously, I went after Barntree with everything I had because I thought he was responsible. And you know who my biggest ally was, who wanted me to try everything until there was nothing more to try? J. P. Arthur. He's got a good record as far as I'm concerned."

She walked toward the cell door as if she was ready to be let out.

"Don't look at his record," Joe said. "Look at his boots."

Becky turned around. "What's that supposed to mean?" she asked.

"The heels of his boots are gold-plated," Joe said.

"Just what Axeblade Pete said about the man he saw hanging around our van right before it caught fire," Frank said.

"Axeblade Pete." Becky gave a small laugh. "Half the time you can't believe him, and the other half, you'd *better not* believe him."

"After this," Frank said, "I'm going to believe every word he says."

"The sheriff is working for Barntree," Joe said emphatically. "Trust me."

Becky shrugged and called for the deputy.

Frank watched her walk down the long hallway and through the open door into the sheriff's office. A moment later, Frank and Joe heard her say, "You did a good job, J.P. I was wrong about those two. I say it's a good thing you pulled their plug as soon as you did."

Frank and Joe looked at each other in their dark cell. "She's not going to help us," Joe said with a low moan.

"I know," Frank said. "We're dead!"

9 On the Trail of Trouble

"I feel like the walls are closing in." Joe paced back and forth across the jail cell. He liked being in a tight spot when it meant danger and the need for quick action. But this tight spot—three slimy-looking walls and a fourth wall of steel bars—was another story.

"Hang in there," Frank said. "We'll think of something." He tried to hear what was going on in the sheriff's office. Had Becky left yet? He couldn't tell. He pressed the side of his face against the cell bars, listening. But only for a moment. A large bug, crawling down one of the bars, walked across his face. Frank jerked his head violently to shake off the bug and stepped back.

Just then, Sheriff Arthur called loudly to his deputies. "Boys, why don't you go on home? We got those kids in a sardine can and don't need to deal with them till tomorrow. I don't mind holding down the fort."

Frank and Joe heard the men gladly accepting the sheriff's offer. The deputies left the office noisily. Then the sheriff spoke again, in a softer voice. "Hope you're not in a big hurry, too, Becky."

Bugs forgotten, Frank leaned against the steel-barred cell door. Joe joined him.

"I locked up the restaurant for the night," Becky said. "And Kwo's getting old enough not to need me around all the time."

"He's a smart little fella, that kid," said the sheriff. "Always got his nose in a book. I've got to say, when he first came to stay with you and Tom, I didn't think he'd fit in around here."

"We all do in time," Becky said.

"It's been a long time since I've been alone with a woman as beautiful as you." Sheriff Arthur's voice got even softer. He added a friendly laugh.

"Nice of you to say that, J.P.," Becky said.

"I used to tell Tom, rest his soul, I used to say right to his face, 'You're a lucky man, Tom.' I hope that doesn't upset you, Becky."

Joe and Frank were motionless, listening. Joe tapped his brother, whispering, "This is beginning to sound like a soap opera."

"Shh," said Frank.

"Becky, I'm not the youngest or the handsomest man in town," said the sheriff.

"No one stays the youngest, handsomest, or prettiest forever, J.P.," Becky said.

"But I'm an important man," the sheriff went on. "I've got a lot of friends, the kind who can make your life wonderful or miserable just by their choosing. Do you know what I mean? Now, if you and I were to get married . . ." He stopped and cleared his throat.

Becky was silent for a minute. Finally she spoke. "J.P., I've got some coffee that's not half-cold and some apple-raisin pie that's not half-bad at the café. What would you say if I brought some over and then we continued this conversation?"

"Sounds great," J. P. Arthur said eagerly.

Joe and Frank heard the front door to the office open and close. "Well, this is just terrific," Joe said finally. "We call the one person in this whole town who doesn't treat us like rabid dogs, and what happens? Not only does she refuse to help us, she wants to bring dessert back for the creep that's framing us!"

Frank didn't answer. His stomach was in knots. If Becky wouldn't help them, then no one in Axeblade would.

A short while later, Becky was back. Frank and Joe leaned forward to listen again.

"That pie is a work of art," the sheriff said.

"You take your coffee black, don't you, J.P.?" asked Becky.

"Nice of you to remember," he said to her.

"Whoa, there. Maybe I'll take one of those packs of sugar after all. This coffee sure is bitter. No offense, Becky, but I haven't had a really good cup of coffee in the café since Tom died."

"I could never get close to a man who complained about my cooking, J.P.," Becky said.

"No, no, I wasn't complaining," the sheriff said quickly. "Maybe it's my tongue. I've just got a funny taste in my mouth."

"J.P., what's going to happen to those boys back there?"

"Don't know," Sheriff Arthur said. He sounded like he was talking with his mouth full. "It's not for me to decide."

"You mean it's for a jury to decide?" asked Becky.

"Yeah," the sheriff said hesitantly. "Yeah, something like that."

"Have some more coffee, J.P."

They kept talking. Sheriff Arthur kept dishing out compliments, and Becky kept urging him to have more pie and coffee.

"He must be eating the whole pie—"

"—at one time," Joe whispered, finishing Frank's thought. "Every time he says something he sounds like his mouth is more and more full, and—"

Crash!

Joe looked at Frank. Something heavy had hit the floor in the outer office.

While the sound of the crash was still echoing, Becky ran down the hallway to their cell. A large key ring jangled in her hand. "Let's go, and I mean fast!" she said, unlocking the cell door.

Frank and Joe followed her silently. There would be time for questions later. Right now was the time for escape.

As they ran through the front office they saw Sheriff Arthur lying on the floor. They ran past him, out the door, and jumped straight into Becky's car. It was a big twenty-year-old sedan with a huge back seat.

"Duck down so no one sees you," Becky said, starting the engine and then roaring out of town. "Where are we going?"

"Let's stop at our van to get what's left of our camping gear," Frank said. "And then take us to Barntree's ranch. We've got to see the tanker trucks tonight."

After a quick stop at Bill Hunt's garage, Becky drove out of town.

As they sped through the night Frank asked Becky, "What happened back there?"

"J.P. took a handful of my sleeping pills in his coffee." Becky's eyes darted left and right, and she kept checking the rearview mirror.

"But why did you change your mind about us?"

Becky shook her head. "I don't know," she said. "I kept thinking about things you and Joe had said. And for the first time in my life, I saw myself as a quitter." She hit the buttons on her door, and all four power windows slid down. The wind was fresh and cool. "I fought for my son, and I fought to keep the café open after Tom died, and I fought Ben Barntree because I thought he was a slow poison for this town. But when people finally began to accept me and Kwo, I stopped fighting. I guess I just became another silent citizen of Axeblade."

"I could hear your voice change when you were talking to the sheriff," Frank said.

"His talk about friends disgusted me," Becky said, keeping her eyes on the road. "He's Barntree's stooge. He must be. All the time I thought he was helping me after Tom died, he was probably spying on me for Barntree. Of course, I can't prove that—any more than I can prove Barntree had Tom killed."

"Well, maybe after tonight we'll be able to prove that the sheriff is really working for Barntree, not for Axeblade," Frank said. "At least I hope we'll have some answers. Right now, all we've got is questions."

Becky stopped the car at the place where Ben Barntree's ranch ended and the national park began. The Hardys got out near the private road they had driven on earlier that day. Frank hadn't noticed it before, but all along the left side of the road there was a fence. It separated Barntree's property from the park.

"I don't know what you think you're going to find, but good luck," Becky said.

"What about you and Kwo?" Frank asked, leaning into the passenger-side window. "What

91

are you going to do when Sheriff Arthur wakes up?"

Becky let out a breath. "Well, we're not going to run away, if that's what you mean," she said. "He can arrest me, I guess—but he'll have a fight on his hands. I promise you that."

She smiled confidently at Frank and Joe.

"Thanks," Frank said. "Thanks for everything." Frank and Joe watched Becky drive away and kept watching until they could no longer see the taillights of her car.

"Now what?" Joe asked.

"We'd better stay out of sight," Frank said.

"That's for sure," Joe said. "But what are we looking for?"

"The toxic dump. That's got to be why we got beaten up the other night. We were in the wrong place at the right time."

"I hate it when you tell me things I already know," Joe said. "It means you're as stumped as I am."

"Anyway, we're in the right place now, I'm sure of that," Frank said. "We just have to figure out what to look for."

"Hey, remember Bill Hunt's message?" Joe said.

"Check the fence," said Frank.

"It's worth a try," his brother answered.

They took out two flashlights and walked over to the fence. Metal posts and metal crossbars seemed to stretch all the way from the main road to the back of the property line. Frank and Joe followed the fence, walking on Barntree's land.

The night air was still, but the woods were noisy with life. The brothers kept their eyes on the fence, the forest, and the dirt road. They saw huge tire tracks on the dirt road, tracks left by the tanker trucks.

"Car!" Joe whispered suddenly.

Frank stopped. He didn't hear anything or see headlights. "Are you sure?"

"Trust me," Joe said, pushing his brother to the ground behind a tree. A minute later Frank saw a light.

The car, coming from Barntree's house, drove slowly down the driveway and turned toward them. A searchlight mounted by the outside mirror flashed this way and that. The car was headed out toward the main road.

When the car had passed, Frank stood up and smiled at his brother. "Close one. Thanks."

They went back to following the fence and the road and the tire tracks. Joe swung his flashlight from side to side, occasionally sweeping the arc of light into the park. Suddenly he saw something familiar—their camping gear.

"Look," Joe said to his brother. "Through the shrubs. It's the spot where we camped the other night."

"That's weird," Frank said. "I didn't notice this fence then, did you?"

"No," Joe replied. "I had no idea we were so close to Barntree's property."

Joe crawled through the fence and tossed their supplies and equipment back over to Frank. He tucked their radio into his pack.

After that they walked for a while on opposite sides of the fence, Frank on Barntree's land and Joe, to his left, in the national park.

"Hold it, Joe," Frank said excitedly. He stopped and aimed his flashlight at the ground. "Look—the road turns to the right, but the tire tracks stop."

Joe's flashlight lit up the earth on his side of the fence. "That's because they start over here."

In the beam of his flashlight, Frank followed the tire tracks. They turned left, away from the road on Barntree's property and toward the metal fence. And they continued on the other side.

"How do they get through?" Joe said, looking at the fence.

"Must be an opening here somewhere," Frank answered.

The two of them felt the fence with their hands, looking for a break, an opening. Finally, with a grunt, Joe simply tried to hoist one of the metal sections. Much to his surprise, it lifted away.

Frank walked through from Barntree's land to the national park, following the tire tracks. Then he and Joe stared at each other.

What they were thinking was horrible, almost too horrible to say out loud.

"The trucks drive *through* here," Frank said. "They drive from Barntree's property *into the park*." His heart was pounding in his chest.

They started following the tire tracks again, deeper into the park. This time they went quickly, half running, not even noticing the weight of their backpacks.

After a while, the forest began to take on an eerie look. The trees were bare of branches, the bushes yellow, dried, and dead. The ground turned from hard and dry to soft and damp.

Then, in the round white circles of their flashlight beams, Frank and Joe saw a dead body. First there was only one—the body of a raccoon, half-decayed. Then they saw two dead squirrels and a few birds.

Worst of all was the sickening smell. The smell of rotting plants and animals—and of something else, too—was almost overpowering.

"I don't think we should go any farther," Frank said.

"The tire tracks keep going," Joe said.

"Forget the tire tracks," Frank said. "We've got to get out of here. It's too dangerous. We're practically standing in the toxic waste dump!"

"And that means," Joe said in a hard voice, "that Barntree isn't dumping the poisons on *his* land. He's dumping them in the national park!"

95

They turned around and quickly walked back up the road.

Suddenly the ground began to rumble. In the distance, headlights and diesel-engine roar began to fill the forest. The tanker trucks were coming!

10 The Secret's Out

"What are we going to do?" Joe said. There was a note of panic in his voice.

"We can hide in the woods, and they'll never know we're here," Frank said. Quickly they moved away from the toxic dump site, running deeper into the woods. The tanker trucks were still on the road leading north—heading toward them. They still had time.

Suddenly Joe grabbed his brother's shoulder and yanked him to a stop. "The fence!" Joe shouted.

"Oh, no," Frank said, realizing they had forgotten to put the removable section of fence back. "They'll know we're here for sure."

It was a race, a contest between them and the

tankers. The Hardys ran as fast as they could toward the fence, while the tanker trucks bumped their way slowly up the dirt road. Their headlights occasionally sparkled through openings between the trees and then disappeared again.

Finally Frank and Joe reached the opening. The trucks were still in the distance.

"Do you remember how it goes?" Frank asked.

"It's dark. Who's going to notice?" Joe answered.

Breathing hard, the two brothers lifted the removable metal section, which they had leaned against the fence. Grunting, they set it in place.

"Good as new," Joe said. "Trust me."

"Let's go back to the dump," Frank said. "I want to see the whole ugly operation so we can tell the police."

"We won't have to *go* to the police, you know," Joe said as they hurried back to the site of the toxic dump. "Sheriff Arthur will come looking for us, for sure."

"Yeah, that's the trouble," Frank agreed. "I guess we'll have to find a way to get to Lawton."

Frank and Joe found a spot close enough to the dump site for them to watch the action, but not too close. They perched on some huge boulders to avoid standing on the chemically saturated ground.

When the silver tankers arrived, a jeep was leading them. The jeep pulled off to the side of

98

the road near the fence, allowing the trucks to go forward, one by one.

A man wearing hip boots got out of the jeep, and in the beam from the jeep's headlights, Frank and Joe saw his face clearly.

"Barntree," Joe whispered. "I'd like to push him into this muck."

Barntree, directing traffic, motioned the first truck to pull up to the clearing. When the truck was in position, the driver got out and unrolled a thick hose that was connected to the body of the tanker. Once the hose was stretched out into the woods, the driver turned a round handle.

Frank and Joe couldn't see what happened next, but they could hear what sounded like the rush of liquid.

"How could he do this?" Joe said. "How could anyone destroy animals and animal habitats and ruin this land, probably forever, with chemicals?"

"I don't know," Frank said. "But we're going to find out all we can before tonight is over."

One truck and then another pulled up, uncoiled its hose, and dumped gallon after gallon of poisonous liquids onto the land. Barntree stood off to the side, clearly in charge but not even needing to give orders. The drivers had obviously done this so often, they all knew exactly what to do.

Suddenly there was movement in the bushes by the Hardys. Frank and Joe held their breaths and

99

readied themselves for a fight. Had one of Barntree's men found them? The bushes shook again. Joe put his hands up and tried to see in the dark. Then into a beam of moonlight stepped a skunk.

Frank and Joe froze, and their hearts raced even faster. They had two choices, but they didn't like either one. They could run, which could mean giving themselves away to Barntree.

Or they could hold very still, and hope the skunk might not spray.

The skunk walked closer to them.

"Come on, pal, give us a break," Joe whispered. "Barntree's over there. You know Ben Barntree—he's probably a cousin of yours."

The skunk instantly turned and ran in the opposite direction, deep into the woods. Frank and Joe stifled a laugh.

When all five tankers had been emptied, the drivers shut off their engines, climbed out of their cabs, and crowded around Barntree.

In the sudden silence Frank and Joe heard every word that Barntree said. "Like clockwork, boys, just like clockwork. You've earned every penny." He took a wad of money out of his pocket and began peeling off bills and paying the men. "I was jumpy about this one, what with those two Eastern teenagers nosing around. But you were in and out of here, and nobody knows a thing."

"Are you sure about that, Ben?" asked one of the drivers.

Barntree's voice changed instantly. It became

cool and gruff. "If you've got something to tell me, tell me straight out. Now."

"Okay, Ben, okay," said the driver. "It's just that the fence was different this time."

"Different?" asked Barntree.

Frank poked his brother in the side.

"One section wasn't put back right," said the driver.

"Well, maybe an animal climbed or ran into it or the wind blew it," Barntree said.

"Huh-uh, Ben," the driver insisted. "It wasn't the way we always put it back. The section was on backward, with the crossbars on the park side, not your side."

"All right, Micky," Barntree said with his usual calm voice. "I think I know who's responsible, and I'll take care of it."

Barntree walked quickly to his jeep, opened the door, and leaned in. Suddenly his CB radio sparked to life. "Breaker. Breaker. This is Ben Barntree calling Outpost One. This is Ben Barntree calling Outpost One."

"Sheriff's Office. I mean, Outpost One," squawked the speaker in Barntree's jeep.

"Who is this?" asked Barntree.

"Deputy Hammer, sir."

"Put J.P. on," Barntree said coolly.

"Can't, Mr. Barntree. He's sleeping."

"Then wake him up!" Barntree was losing his self-control.

"Can't, Mr. Barntree. I didn't mean he had gone to sleep on purpose. I meant he's been drugged or something. He's out like a burned-out light bulb. He sent us home early, but I came back to get something, and I found him. Now I can't bring him around."

"What about your two prisoners?" Barntree asked.

There was a long silence, long enough for Frank and Joe to begin to feel lightheaded. Finally the deputy's voice came back on the radio.

"Well, sir, they seem to be gone."

Barntree pounded the side of his jeep with his fist. Then he seemed to pull himself together. "Deputy Hammer, you listen to me."

"Yes, sir."

"And if you think you can't remember every word I say, then you get someone else to listen for you, because I expect everything I say to be followed to the letter."

"Yes, sir," said the nervous voice on the CB speaker.

"First of all, I want you to contact Phoenix Dawson, Robbie McCoy, and Sly Wilkins, and tell them to meet me at my ranch in twenty minutes. Then I want you to form a posse, a real old-fashioned posse. And I want you to take this posse out and search every square inch of this county until you find those two boys. And then you bring them to me. Understand? Hunt them down like dogs. I don't care what they look like when you bring them to me—but bring them. Tonight!"

11 On the Run

Frank and Joe couldn't believe it. A sheriff's posse looking for them! It sounded like a scene from a bad movie. But it wasn't.

"We've got to move," Joe said. "And *now*. While it's still dark."

"Sure, but where?" Frank asked. "Those guys probably know every inch around here, even in the dark."

"True," Joe said. "But they don't know we're *here*. We could have gone anywhere. Let's at least get away from this spot and try to find some place to hide. Maybe we could make it to Lawton."

"It's too far," Frank said quietly.

They watched the tanker trucks pull away from the dump site, followed by Barntree. The silence after they'd gone gave Frank and Joe the feeling that they had the whole park to themselves. It was a good feeling, but they knew it wouldn't last.

"Let's get going," Frank said.

They walked quickly through the darkness, not daring to use their flashlights, and let their instincts guide their actions. The darkness intensified everything: the sound of branches snapping under their feet, the weight and balance of their backpacks, and especially the smells in the air. When the wind shifted, the clean scent of the pine forest was replaced by the odor of decay from the toxic dump.

Joe took the lead and set the pace. They walked steadily, not talking, saving their energy. After a while they stopped to rest. Leaning his back against a tree trunk, Frank felt the sweat soaking his shirt. Joe, beside him, suddenly shivered.

"They're in the park, looking for us now," he said, taking a sip from his canteen. "I can feel it."

"Do you think they'll split up or come at us as a group?" asked Frank. "Maybe we could overpower them one-on-one in the dark." Then he shrugged. "Barntree won't take that chance. He'll—"

Frank's voice was drowned in the roar of motors that seemed to fill the dark woods. The glow of lights, moving fast, flashed somewhere to the Hardys' left. Joe and Frank dropped to their knees and crawled forward.

They were on a rise. And fifty feet below them, two vehicles—a jeep and a van—bounced along a twisting dirt road.

Frank waited until the glow of the taillights disappeared around a curve and then said, "That looked like Barntree and Robbie McCoy."

"Did you see what was on top of the van?" Joe said, his voice just a whisper.

Frank shook his head.

"It looked like a microwave dish," Joe whispered. "It's a parabolic microphone. Very powerful, very sensitive, perfect for tracking and hunting. We've got to be very quiet now. They'll be listening to every move we make."

Quickly, and silently, they slipped into their backpack harnesses. As they were about to move on they heard footsteps in the woods, footsteps coming closer.

Joe held up one finger—meaning he heard only one person.

The two brothers separated so they could come at the attacker from two different directions.

As the footsteps drew nearer the Hardys heard another sound. At first, Frank and Joe couldn't tell what it was. A half moan, half mutter. Then the noise grew louder, and clearer. They heard words, repeated over and over.

"Mommy . . . Daddy . . . Mommy . . . Daddy . . . Mommy . . . Daddy."

"Psst! Hey!" Frank said in a loud whisper. "We're over here."

A thin arm pushed branches aside, and a face,

wide-eyed and scratched by branches, stared at Frank and Joe. Their "attacker" was a boy about four years old, with yellow hair and large eyes. He was wearing pajamas.

"Hi," Frank whispered.

The boy didn't say anything.

"He's in shock," Joe said.

"What are you doing out here?" Frank asked.

"Mommy . . . Daddy . . . Mommy . . . Daddy," the little boy whined like a broken record.

"Shh," Joe said, thinking about Robbie McCoy and the powerful microphone on his van.

"He's lost and totally scared," Frank said. "He must have wandered away from his parents' campsite." He knelt down to be at eye level with the boy. "What's your name?" he asked. "Are you hungry? Thirsty? We've got some food. Come here." Frank's voice was quiet, coaxing, patient. He took off his backpack to find some food.

"Frank, what are we going to do with him? We can't leave him here, and we can't take him with us."

Frank looked at the boy and at his brother. "Everything's going to be okay," he said.

The boy stepped toward them, and his hand closed on Frank's. First Frank gave him his canteen to drink from. Then he found some dried fruit in his pack.

"Drink slowly," Joe said.

"What's your name? Mine's Frank, and this is my brother, Joe."

"Cory," said the boy.

106

"Have you been lost a long time?" Joe asked.

"I saw a squirrel," said the little boy. "I was following the squirrel."

The Hardys peered into the darkness, hoping to see someone or hear the boy's parents calling. But they realized that the family campsites might not be nearby. Cory looked as if he'd been walking for a long time.

From the road below came the sound of a vehicle screeching to a stop.

"I hear a truck!" Cory shouted excitedly. "Mommy! Daddy!"

Joe quickly clamped his hand over Cory's mouth. "Shhh!" he warned. "Those are our friends. We're playing a game with them."

"Come on." Frank took the little boy's hand. "Let's go find your parents."

They started through the trees, but Cory was too slow. So Joe picked him up and ran, carrying the boy against his shoulder. Tree branches slapped at them, like arms trying to grab them. They soon came to a narrow trail and pounded along it as fast as they could.

When they thought they'd gone far enough to be safe for a while, Frank and Joe slowed down, gasping for breath. Joe put Cory back on the ground. The little boy looked at them with curiosity on his face.

"That really wasn't your parents, believe me," Frank said between deep breaths. "Let's keep looking."

But every path they followed in the woods

seemed to lead straight to Robbie McCoy's van or Ben Barntree's jeep. Barntree and McCoy apparently circling through the park, seemed to be everywhere.

"Maybe *we're* walking in circles," Joe said.

At last they came to a place where the trees parted on the edge of a clearing. On the other side of the flat clearing was the base of the mountains that took up much of one corner of the park.

"I'm tired," Cory said, beginning to cry. "I want my mommy."

"Frank, if we stay in the park looking for his parents, we're going to get caught," Joe said. "This is a no-win situation."

"Maybe not," Frank said. He took a deep breath and then shouted at the top of his lungs. "Ben Barntree, come and find us!" He tried it again—even louder.

"What are you doing?" Joe said. "They'll be here any minute!"

"Trust me," Frank said, smiling. Then he knelt down to talk to Cory. "Listen, Cory, Joe and I have to go somewhere. But our friends will be here very soon. You've got to stay right here and wait for them. Tell them you're lost, and they'll take you to your parents."

Joe picked up on his brother's plan. "All you have to do, Cory, is yell, yell loudly, yell anything you want—a song, your name, anything. And they'll come here and find you."

"Don't be afraid, okay?" asked Frank.

Cory nodded.

"Why can't I go with you?" Cory asked.

"Because we're supposed to be somewhere else, and we're late already," Frank said. "The people who find you are going to ask you some questions about us, and you tell them everything you remember. That's important, okay? It's part of the game."

"Including which way we went?" Joe wanted to know.

"Yes," said Frank. "Especially that. Now you start yelling, Cory."

Joe smiled as he caught on to his brother's plan. Cory would tell Barntree's men that the Hardys were heading toward the main road. But really they were going to double back and go in the other direction. A much safer plan than expecting Cory to lie about which direction they took.

Frank gave his flashlight to Cory and turned it on. Then he led his brother back into the woods. They went south, *away* from the mountain.

When they were out of sight, they changed direction and headed north. Then they found a spot where they could still see Cory. They hid themselves well and waited. It was only a matter of minutes before Barntree and McCoy showed up.

"What if Barntree doesn't want to take time to help the kid?" Joe whispered in the dark.

"He won't want to," Frank said. "But I don't think he'll leave Cory there. Just watch. I'll bet he gets on his CB real fast."

Frank was right. They watched as Barntree went to his jeep and pulled the CB microphone to his mouth. A few minutes later, just as Frank had thought, a park ranger showed up and put Cory in his own car.

Joe gave Frank a thumbs-up sign, and they hit the trail once more. In a short time, they reached the mountain and started climbing its wide, rocky base. They climbed until their legs and shoulders ached. It was exhausting, but at least from up high they'd be able to see the posse coming before the posse saw them.

The moon was high in the sky.

"What do you say we get some sleep?" Frank finally said.

At the first plateau they reached, several hundred feet from the bottom of the mountain, they spread their bedrolls out on the flat but rocky ground. They had no fire to warm them or protect them that night, and they didn't get a good look at their surroundings. But they were too tired to care. They just wanted to sleep.

In the morning, however, just after sunrise, Joe woke up with a start. Was he dreaming about an earthquake? It seemed like a dream at first— until he realized that some pebbles were rolling onto his face.

Then, in one terrible moment as he looked up at the mountain, Joe wished they had chosen their campsite more carefully. The ground above him was moving!

"Rock slide!" Joe called, trying to wake his brother, who was sleeping soundly.

But it was too late. Rocks and boulders of all sizes were tumbling over one another, rushing down the mountain toward Joe and Frank!

12 Posse Problems

"Frank!" Joe yelled as he scrambled out of his own sleeping bag.

Above the Hardy brothers' camp, a few huge rocks and a shower of smaller ones bounced and crashed against one another, picking up speed. One of them would be enough to crush them. The entire rock slide would bury them forever.

Frank woke up just in time to see the wall of stones and dirt coming his way. Then a rock the size of a tennis ball flew off the ridge and glanced off the side of his head. He swayed a little as blood rushed to the wound. Then he collapsed, face first, and blacked out.

Joe sprang toward his brother, coughing in the clouds of dust the rock slide was creating.

Dodging smaller stones, Joe grabbed Frank under the arms and started to drag him away.

But where? Around the curve of the mountain Joe saw a small cave, protected by walls of solid rock. With a great effort, he dragged Frank across the plateau to the cave.

An instant later he heard the bigger rocks tumble full-force onto the campsite. The ground shook. Other stones loosened in the fall became part of the slide. The rock slide lasted for more than a minute. When the noise stopped, Joe looked out from the cave. The entire pile of stones had landed exactly where he and Frank had been sleeping.

Joe turned to his brother and checked the bruise on Frank's head. There was a small cut—a little blood streaked Frank's brown hair—and a large lump had begun to form. Joe wiped away the blood with his bandanna. Frank didn't appear to be badly hurt, but he was unconscious. Joe wasn't sure whether he should try to rouse Frank or let him come around naturally. Joe decided to wait.

The morning was finally quiet, the way a morning on a mountain plateau is supposed to be. In the stillness, waiting for his brother to wake up, Joe had time to think about how the plans he and Frank had made for their camping vacation had been ruined. "By Ben Barntree, the all-American polluter," Joe muttered aloud, and he wondered if Barntree had hunted them all night through the national park.

As a soft wind started to blow Frank came to. His brown eyes opened but didn't focus for a minute. "What happened?" he asked, turning his head toward Joe.

"That was our morning wake-up call. Even the mountains in Axeblade aren't friendly," Joe said. "A rock zapped you in the head when you weren't looking. I dragged you over here."

Frank felt the tender lump above his right ear and winced. "How long was I unconscious?"

"Not long," Joe said.

"Well, thanks to you, I didn't lose any body parts," Frank said, looking at his arms and legs.

Joe grinned. "It was a choice between saving my new backpack or my older brother. So I thought I'd give you a break."

They smiled at each other. Okay. Things were back to normal. They'd just dodged a rock slide, and Frank had gotten his brain temporarily scrambled. Now it was time to get back to business.

"We lost all our equipment," Joe said.

Frank stood up, and together they walked over to the remains of their camp. There was nothing to find. Everything—equipment and supplies—was buried under a ton of rocks.

"No food and no water," Frank said. "We won't make it over the mountain. And we can't stay here, either, with no supplies. The sun's getting hot already."

"We can climb back down the mountain," Joe said, "but it's a safe bet that Ben Barntree has formed a welcoming committee for us down there."

Frank nodded. "But he can't be everywhere at once. Let's try going around and then sneaking down the other side."

It didn't sound like the best plan to either brother. But it *did* sound like the only plan. So for an hour, while the sun slowly climbed in the sky, Frank and Joe followed paths that they hoped would bring them to the other side of Mount Regina. Some paths were wide, and the walking was easy. Others were narrow. A wrong step could send them sliding over the edge of the ridge.

For some time they had been following one such narrow path that clung to the side of the mountain. Suddenly the path ended. It had been torn away by falling rocks. All that remained was a thin ledge, four inches wide, running along the wall of rock. Below was nothing for five hundred feet and then a floor of rocks and sand.

"We're going to have to walk along that ledge," Joe said.

"No way," Frank said. "There's got to be another option." He was still feeling shaky from his encounter with the falling rock.

Joe tossed a stone from where they were standing to where the path got wider again after thirty feet of nothingness. "I can only think of one other option," he said.

"What?" asked Frank.

"Learn to fly."

Frank laughed.

"We can make it," Joe said. "I'll go first, and then you just do what I do."

"Okay," Frank said. "Unless you fall and splatter yourself on the rocks down there. Then I'll try something different."

Joe laughed. "Do that." He stepped forward onto the narrow ledge and inched along, walking sideways. His toes were pointed into the mountain, and he leaned his weight inward so that his arms and chest dragged across the stone as he walked.

"The rock's sharp. It cuts your arms," Joe said. He was breathing quickly as he took small sideways steps.

He took another step, and a small part of the ledge gave way, sending dirt and stones on a five-hundred-foot drop.

"Watch out for that step," Joe said. He even tried to smile, but his face was stiff with fear.

Frank held his breath for his brother, as if it was on the ledge instead of Joe. For someone who could run so quickly, it was taking Joe Hardy a long time to walk this thirty feet. Finally Joe stepped to the solid path on the other side of the thirty-foot gap.

"Your turn," he said encouragingly.

Frank stepped onto the ledge but didn't move. He wasn't thinking about falling. He was getting his balance, feeling the face of the red stone mountain. As Joe had said, the rock was sharp to the touch, yet it was smooth, too. Centuries of wind had blown away its hard edges. Frank knew, as he dragged his feet, taking one step, then another and another, that a strong wind now in the wrong direction would probably blow him away like a leaf.

"What's that noise?" Frank froze in the middle of the narrow ledge.

"I don't hear anything," Joe answered.

"*Whupp-whupp-whupp*," Frank said.

"Probably your heart," Joe said. "It's the sound of total fear. Come on. You're halfway across."

"No. I hear something else. It's getting closer." Frank's face was wet with sweat.

Then the *whupp-whupp-whupp* Frank had heard so faintly turned into a loud pounding sound. Joe looked up at the sky just as a helicopter came around the mountain, swooping toward them. It hovered over them. The wind from its whirling rotors kicked up dust that stung Frank's face as he clung to the side of the mountain.

"Come on, Frank! We've got to get out of here," Joe called above the noise. "That's not a rescue chopper. It's got the B-Bar-B brand painted on the side!"

Frank started moving again slowly, scraping his feet across the ledge.

Joe, watching the helicopter, saw the door slide open. His heart raced when he saw the pilot lean out of the chopper, some kind of pistol in his hand. "Come on, Frank. Go for it!" he shouted. "Hurry!"

Finally Frank reached the other side of the

gap. Joe grabbed his arm and pulled him onto the path.

Just then a trail of red smoke flew from the gun the pilot was holding and trailed to the ground near Frank and Joe. A puffy red cloud began to hang in the air above them.

"Flare gun," Frank said. "He's showing Barntree where we are."

"Then let's get out of here!" Joe said.

They moved as quickly as they could, but the early afternoon sun was pounding them, and the helicopter kept following. Some of the trails they took led nowhere. When they doubled back, they weren't certain which way they were headed.

Finally Frank stopped to catch his breath. When he looked down the mountain, his heart sank. The chase was over. Barntree, Robbie McCoy, and Sly Wilkins were directly below. Frank tapped Joe and pointed in that direction.

"Look. They're coming up after us," he said.

The three cowboys were forty feet below. At the rate they were climbing, it wouldn't take them long to catch up with Frank and Joe.

"It's a squeeze play," Joe said. "The helicopter chases us from behind, and we run right into Barntree coming the other way."

"What do you want to do?" Frank asked. "Try cutting back?"

But before Joe could answer, there was a shower of stones and dirt from above. A man slid down the mountainside to land on his feet behind Frank and Joe.

118

"You can't go back, buckaroos," said Phoenix Dawson, grinning victoriously. He held a rope in one hand as he dusted off his jeans and shirt with the other. "This little game of cat and mouse is over. You just keep walking until we meet Mr. Barntree."

"We can take him, Frank," Joe said, getting ready to fight.

But Phoenix answered first. "Maybe," he said. "And just maybe one of you will go sliding off this mountain. Smart thing to do is go to Mr. Barntree. He just wants to talk. That's all."

"If he just wants to talk, he could use the phone," Frank said.

Phoenix Dawson smiled, showing a mouthful of crooked teeth. He motioned with his head for the Hardys to start walking.

There wasn't much choice. Joe and Frank were outnumbered and trapped. So they followed the path Phoenix pointed out. It was steep and fast, and at the end stood Ben Barntree, with Robbie McCoy and Sly Wilkins.

"Okay, Ben," Robbie said. "We got 'em. Now let's get 'em back to jail."

But Ben Barntree didn't answer Robbie. He didn't even look at him. He looked as if, as far as he was concerned, there were only three people on the planet: himself and Frank and Joe Hardy.

"You boys were trouble when you *didn't* know anything," Barntree said calmly. "Now that you do know, you leave me no choice."

"What do we know?" Joe challenged him.

119

Barntree answered in his calm, powerful manner. "You know about the dump. I know you do. I found your trail." He shook his head at them gently, as if he were scolding a small grandson for dropping cookie crumbs on the rug. Then, for the first time, Frank and Joe heard Ben Barntree sound tough. "Bring 'em," he commanded Phoenix and Sly. Phoenix pushed Frank and Joe forward.

"Wait a minute, Ben," Robbie said. "You promised we'd call the sheriff."

"Now, Robbie," Barntree said over his shoulder. "I've already got *two* problems to deal with. Don't give me a third." He turned to face the young rancher.

"You understand, don't you, Rob? We can't have them telling people about the dump. There's no choice. They've got to die."

13 The End?

"Hold it, Ben." Robbie McCoy's voice was shaky. Barntree, Sly, and Phoenix stared at him as if he were the enemy. "You're talking straight-out murder."

"These two know enough to send us away for a long time, Robbie," said Barntree. "It's us or them." His voice was calm, but there was a definite threat in the way he stood rigidly blocking the path.

Robbie backed away from Barntree and paced nervously. "There's got to be another way. Pay them off. That's what this is all about, isn't it? Money? Who wouldn't want to be a millionaire?"

Frank and Joe looked around. They were in the middle of a wilderness with four lawless men. It wasn't anything like a courtroom, but they *knew* they were on trial.

Sly Wilkins moved over to Robbie's side of the path. He took off his mirrored sunglasses. Without them, he looked tired. "Mr. Barntree, I don't have any use for these two, but I don't want to be involved in killing."

Barntree looked at young Phoenix Dawson. "Anything you say, Mr. Barntree," Phoenix said.

For the next several seconds, Barntree was silent.

"Okay," he finally said with a smile. He relaxed his shoulders. "I got carried away. We'll find another way."

Robbie McCoy was relieved. "Good," he said.

Once it was decided, everyone seemed to relax, especially Frank and Joe. They needed time to come up with an escape plan, and they had just been given a little more of it.

"But these two are still trouble," Barntree said as they walked down the path. He put his arm around Robbie's shoulder. "We've got another delivery tonight, the last one this month. Help me tie up these boys down in my basement. Then we can decide what to do with them tomorrow."

Frank and Joe were forced into Robbie's van for the ride back to Barntree's ranch. Phoenix rode with Barntree in the jeep. Sly sat on a saddle in the back of the van, watching Frank and Joe. He'd picked up a wrench somewhere, and he slapped it on his palm to warn them not to try anything.

122

Nobody said a word. Then Robbie spoke up. "Well, say something," he said to the Hardys.

"What do you want us to say?" asked Joe.

"Say you're sorry you didn't get out of town when we gave you the chance," Robbie said. "Say you're not going to tell anybody anything. Say thanks for me saving your necks."

"How could you do it?" was all Frank said. "How could you dump millions of gallons of poison into this beautiful land?"

"Shut up!" Robbie shouted. He glanced at Sly. "I hope I did the right thing."

They rode in silence until Robbie pulled into Barntree's drive. Barntree pulled in behind him.

"Let's go," Sly said, still holding the wrench.

As the Hardys got out of Robbie's van, a woman walked down the drive from the house.

"Afternoon, Mrs. Barntree," Sly called.

Mrs. Barntree was a small woman with curly gray hair. She wore a shiny flower-printed dress, white socks, and slippers. She gave Barntree a quick kiss on the cheek and turned to the Hardys with a welcoming smile.

Does she know what's going on? Frank wondered.

She looked at Frank and Joe with such kind eyes that Frank sensed she didn't. He wondered how Barntree was going to explain tying up two teenagers in their basement. He also wondered if she might help them escape.

"Are you hungry, dear?" Mrs. Barntree asked her husband.

123

"I will be when I'm done here," he said.

"Is there anything I can do to help?" she asked softly.

"No, Margaret. We're just going to tie 'em up in the basement for the night," Barntree told her.

"The basement's good, Ben," said Mrs. Barntree. "Nobody'll hear them down there if they scream."

Frank's heart sank. So much for counting on her help, he thought. If he and Joe were going to escape, they'd have to do it on their own.

Sly and Phoenix grabbed Frank and Joe by the arms and pushed them into the basement of Barntree's ranch house. The Hardys studied the room quickly. Where were its weak points?

The basement was cool and damp. A stale smell hung like a cloud. No doors. No windows. The only way out was the way they'd come in—down the stairs. Frank and Joe made a mental note of the light switch and the basement door lock.

The basement had a concrete floor and dark wood paneling. It was one big room, divided up into different areas. One section was laid out as Barntree's office, with a desk, telephone, and file cabinets. Another was filled with boxes. Another was used for storing old furniture.

From the pile of furniture, Barntree dragged out a couple of heavy, tall-backed oak chairs. Then Sly and Phoenix held the Hardys in place while Barntree tied them up. Robbie paced. A few minutes later Mrs. Barntree brought down three glasses of iced tea. Two had straws in them.

When Barntree was done, Frank and Joe were sitting back-to-back, about three feet apart. They could hardly move their arms or legs. Mrs. Barntree held a glass of iced tea with a straw in front of Joe. He sipped greedily. Then she did the same with Frank.

"Okay. They're out of our hair. And we're not going to deal with them until tomorrow. Right, Ben?" Robbie McCoy said once more before he left.

"That's what we agreed, Robbie," said Ben Barntree, sounding like a patient father. "You boys come here and meet me in the morning."

Phoenix and Sly stomped up the basement stairs, and Robbie reluctantly followed. When they were gone, Mrs. Barntree's warm smile faded. "Why'd you bring them here, Ben?" she asked sharply.

"Robbie, Sly, Phoenix—they've got no stomach for killing," Barntree answered.

Killing? Frank's stomach knotted at the word. Barntree took a long drink of his iced tea.

"Well, I guess that's just what's wrong with young people today," said Mrs. Barntree. "Phoenix and Sly are nice boys, but they don't like to finish what they start."

"Guess I'm going to have to do it myself," Barntree said.

The words knocked the air out of Frank and Joe, as if they'd been hit with a boulder from the rock slide. "You can't kill us," Joe said. "People will know."

125

"I'm up to my neck in toxic poisons. I can't do anything else," Barntree said. "See, I had this town wrapped up. Then you two came along and threw everything out of kilter."

"When, dear?" Mrs. Barntree asked.

"Tonight," Barntree said with a decisive nod of his head. "I'll take them back up the mountain after the dumping is over. Then I'll throw them over a cliff. Next morning, I'll say they escaped, and we'll hunt for them again. This time all we'll find is a couple of broken bodies on the rocks."

"Sounds like you've had a lot of practice," Frank said. "Is that what you did to Tom Waldo?"

Barntree's eyes narrowed. "You shouldn't have said that. In fact, you boys should have just taken the beating we gave you as a warning and gotten clean out of Axeblade. But no—you had to snoop around, just like Tom Waldo. And now you're going to die, just like he did."

"Becky knows you killed him," Frank said, playing for time. "And she'll know you killed us. You won't get away with it."

"I get away with anything I want," Barntree said with a calm smile. "I control the bank and own half the property in this town. Jobs are too scarce for people to cross me. They know I'll foreclose on 'em—take their houses and businesses away, just like that." He snapped his fingers.

"Tom Waldo wasn't afraid of you," Joe said.

"Yeah—he thought he was pretty big. Owned that café, rode around on that old motorcycle of

126

his." Barntree laughed softly. "But motorcycles are dangerous. And he should have been more careful with his."

"What do you mean?" Frank asked.

"That's how I knew Tom had found the dump. I saw tire tracks from his Harley in the mud."

With that, Barntree started up the stairs, with his wife close behind. At the top, they turned out the light and closed the door.

With no windows, the cellar was pitch black. Frank and Joe couldn't see each other, or anything that would help them to escape. They couldn't even see the ropes binding their hands and feet.

"Got any ideas?" Joe asked softly.

"Yeah," Frank said. "Next time we take a vacation, let's go to Hawaii."

Joe barely laughed. The ropes around his wrists were already beginning to hurt. "Let's try to move our chairs together," he said.

Frank began to rock back and forth in his chair. He was trying to rock the chair off its front legs enough to scoot it. But the oak chair was heavy, and the way Barntree had tied him made it almost impossible to move.

After an hour of trying, Frank and Joe had managed to move within inches of each other. But they still couldn't free themselves or reach for the other's ropes. The dark was their greatest enemy.

"I give up," Joe said in frustration. "Help! Someone get us out of here! Help!"

Suddenly the lights snapped on. Frank and Joe froze. In the light, they saw that they were now only inches apart. Barntree was coming—he'd notice the difference for sure! He'd know that they were trying to escape! And *then* what would he do?

The footsteps on the carpeted stairway came down slowly. There wasn't time for Frank and Joe to try to move away from each other.

Joe held his breath. Step . . . step . . . Mrs. Barntree's socks and slippers came into view. As she walked across the basement she looked at Frank and Joe blankly. "Just came down to get something from the freezer for dinner."

She went to the freezer, took out two steaks, then walked back upstairs.

As soon as the door closed, Joe twisted his body, moving his chair as quickly as he could toward his brother.

"She left the light on!" Joe whispered. "That's our break."

"You okay?" Frank said.

"Yeah—just angry," Joe said in a cold, determined voice. He stretched, trying to get to Frank's ropes. But it was no use. He couldn't move his fingers enough to undo the knots.

"I've got a knife in my pocket," Frank said. "I almost got it to fall out in the dark. See if you can grab it."

Joe inched his chair into position, with his back nearer to Frank's side. That way he could use his hands to reach for the knife. He strained against his own ropes, reaching.

"Got it!" he said.

"Don't drop it," Frank said.

"Now I've got to figure out how to open it one-handed," Joe said.

Just then the door opened again, and heavy footsteps came down the stairs. Barntree saw the two chairs pushed close together.

"That's not where I put you two," he said impatiently. He walked toward them and, with two strong kicks, knocked over Joe and Frank's chairs.

They crashed onto their sides, landing against the floor with full force.

"That'll fix you," Barntree said.

"Barntree!" Joe called as the man walked away. "When you're dumping all those poisons in the park tonight—have a *big* drink of them on us."

"I'll be back for you later" was all Barntree said. At the top of the stairs he turned out the light and slammed the door.

Frank and Joe waited for the gloomy silence to fall around them again.

"Still have the knife?" Frank asked.

"Move your chair over here, and let's get this thing open," Joe said impatiently.

With more struggling and twisting, Frank and Joe were able to get the knife open and get into position to use it. But they dropped the knife

129

twice. It took them several hours to get the job done.

Joe sawed furiously at the ropes on Frank's hands. "I'm loose," Frank finally said.

A few minutes later, they were both free, flexing their arms and legs to get the circulation going again. Frank turned the light back on.

"It's late. Barntree's probably gone already," Frank said, checking his watch. "We've got to get out of here."

"Yeah, but if we want to stop the dumping, we're going to need some backup in the park," Joe said. He was eyeing an old CB radio on Barntree's desk. It was dusty and unplugged. "Do you think it works?"

"Who would we call?"

"Kwo," they both said at the same time.

"Right. He said he listens to the truckers on dump nights," Frank said. "We'll have to be careful about what we say, but it's our only chance. Check the door to be sure no one's coming."

Joe walked up the basement stairs to try the door. "Locked," he reported when he came back. "I can hear Mrs. Barntree listening to some game show on TV."

"She's probably watching 'Name That Toxin,'" Frank joked. He plugged in the AC adapter of the CB unit and turned it on. "Breaker, breaker," Frank said into the microphone. "This is the Harley Hog, and I'm looking for a half-pint named Kwo. Any good buddies out there know Kwo, tell him I'm on channel fourteen."

They listened, but all they heard was a lot of static interrupted occasionally by scrambled voices. Who was out there in Axeblade tonight? Was Kwo listening? Was Barntree? They had to hope that Kwo would recognize Frank's voice— and that Barntree *wouldn't.*

Frank repeated his message into the CB. Still no answer.

"What are you going to tell him if he answers?" Joe asked.

"I'm going to give him directions that will lead him here," Frank replied.

Suddenly they heard a voice coming over the radio. "This is Kwo," the young voice said. He came on a little too loud. Frank had to turn the volume down quickly.

"Okay, good buddy," Frank said. "Go ahead."

"I'm looking for the Harley Hog," Kwo said.

"You found him," Frank said.

"Who are you?" asked Kwo.

"Remember my bike? It's a 1965 Harley Sportster. Got it now?"

Frank looked at his brother. Would Kwo recognize Frank's voice? Would he keep his cool and not reveal who Frank was in case Barntree was listening, too?

"What do you want, Harley Hog?" Kwo asked. "I remember you." His voice was perfect—calm and friendly.

131

"I need some *help* with math homework," Frank said. "It's a problem I can't work out."

"What kind of problem?" Kwo asked.

"It's one of those time and place problems," Frank said. "You know—getting people to a certain place by the right time."

"You mean time and distance," said Kwo.

"Right," said Frank. "It's the one we're supposed to have done tonight. I'll read it to you. It says, 'how long would it take a group of people to drive nine miles west and then three miles south and follow a winding road that's about three miles long?'"

"Where are these people coming from?" asked Kwo. "Close by? Far away? That's part of the distance formula."

"If I'm reading the problem right, they're coming from somewhere like the next town," said Frank.

Kwo was quiet for a minute. Then he spoke up again. "What time do they have to be there? That affects their speed, you know," Kwo said.

"About midnight," Frank said. "And these guys can really drive fast, fast as a *smokey*. Do you think you can work that problem out for me?"

Before Kwo could answer, the basement door opened. Frank snapped off the CB immediately. He and Joe slipped under the basement stairs.

14 Scene of the Crime

Frank and Joe waited under the stairs, wishing they'd had time to flip off the lights. Who was coming this time? Whoever it was, the Hardys would give them a surprise.

Joe pointed to himself and to Frank. The silent message was, "We both jump him to make sure we take him out."

From under the steps they could hear the footsteps, but they couldn't see the feet because the stairs were closed.

"Oh, dear." The voice was Mrs. Barntree's.

"Okay," Joe whispered. "She's seen the empty chairs and the cut rope. Time to move!"

Frank and Joe started to come out from behind the stairs. They were ready to spring, two guys against a middle-aged woman. Piece of cake.

"Now!" Frank yelled.

He and Joe jumped forward, then froze. Mrs. Barntree had a shotgun!

"Duck!" Joe shouted.

Both Hardys hit the floor behind the stairway just as Mrs. Barntree pulled the trigger. The loud explosion shook the basement walls. Shotgun pellets scattered everywhere. Boxes and fragments of the stairway seemed to explode into a thousand pieces.

Then it was quiet. Too quiet. Frank and Joe peeked out. Mrs. Barntree was lying on her back. The shotgun was on the floor at her feet.

"Is she hurt?" Frank asked.

"The kick of the gun knocked her over," Joe whispered.

Joe made a diving slide across the concrete floor just as Mrs. Barntree started to sit up. He reached the gun first. Joe quickly stood up, opened the barrel of the shotgun, and took out the shells. Both of them had been fired. The gun was useless now.

"What are you going to do?" Mrs. Barntree asked. She didn't seem scared. She was as cool as her husband.

"We're going to tie you up," Frank said, picking up lengths of rope from the floor.

He handed the ropes to Joe and hurried back to the CB. "Breaker, breaker. Kwo, this is the Harley Hog. Are you still there?"

Static. Frank tried again. "Kwo, are you still there?"

"He's gone," said Joe. "Do you think he got our message?"

Frank shrugged and came over to help his brother. They tied Mrs. Barntree to one of the big wooden chairs.

"My husband will go crazy if you hurt me," she said coldly.

Frank stopped and looked at her as though she had just told him an important secret. He turned to his brother. "Get to the dump," he said. "Do what you can to trap them at the site. If Kwo is bringing the police from Lawton, we want them to catch Barntree in the act."

"What about you?" said Joe.

"I'll take care of tying up some loose ends around here," Frank said with a smile.

"What are you going to do?" Joe asked.

"Wait and see," Frank said, grinning.

Joe took the stairs two at a time and raced out of Barntree's house. He sprinted up the road toward the national park.

As he ran he thought of a plan. The truck . . . the fence . . . it should work, as long as Barntree parked his jeep exactly where he had parked it the night before.

The silver tanker trucks, gleaming in the moonlight, were just arriving when Joe reached the dump site. He smiled when he saw Barntree's jeep. It was parked where Joe wanted it to be—by the metal fence. And Barntree was sitting behind the wheel with the headlights trained on the dump site in the woods.

"Okay," Joe said softly. "So far so good."

Joe's plan was simple. He would wait for Barntree to leave the jeep. Then he'd jump in and drive the jeep into the space that led into the dump site. By leaving the vehicle crossways, right where the piece of fence belonged, he would be blocking the tankers from getting back out!

It would work. It had to. The trees in the woods grew close together, so the tankers couldn't drive around the jeep to escape from the dump site. They'd be trapped—and he and Frank would have the proof they needed! If only the police arrived in time . . .

Joe waited ten, fifteen, twenty minutes. Why hadn't Frank come yet? Why didn't Kwo and the police show up? Why didn't Barntree get out of his jeep?

One by one, the tanker trucks unreeled their hoses and started pumping gallon after gallon of hideous poisons into the ground.

The smell was blowing toward Joe. He thought he was going to throw up.

What was keeping Frank?

Finally Joe couldn't wait any longer for Frank, or for Kwo, or for Barntree to leave his jeep.

He moved quickly through the trees, around bushes. His eyes darted everywhere. The truck drivers were taking care of their loads. They wouldn't see him. Not yet.

136

As he came closer to Barntree's jeep Joe slowed to a watchful crawl. Down low, finally on his knees, creeping closer to the driver's side where Barntree was sitting.

Joe crouched right under the door handle and the open window of the jeep.

Okay, Joe, he thought to himself. Make it fast, make it noisy—surprise is everything.

He took a deep breath, and with a frantic, crazed scream, he jerked open the jeep door. In one quick, violent move, he grabbed Barntree and started to jerk him out of the seat by the neck.

Their eyes met—the older man's surprised and confused, Joe's angry and determined.

Joe's adrenaline was pumping power to every muscle. He pulled so hard he practically sent Barntree flying. The man tumbled to the ground. When he started to stand up, Joe gave him a quick kick to the stomach. It knocked the wind out of Barntree and sent him back down again.

That's all the time Joe needed. He hopped in the jeep and slammed the door shut to drive away.

His left foot tromped on the clutch as his right hand reached for the ignition key. The key? The key wasn't in the ignition!

Suddenly the jeep door swung open, and before Joe could duck, a fist hit him in the jaw. It sent him flying backward. His head hit the passenger door of the jeep. Then Barntree grabbed

Joe's legs and started to drag him out, just as Joe had done to Barntree a minute earlier.

Joe's head was throbbing, but his instincts were still strong. He bent his knees and straightened them quickly, landing a two-footed kick right in Barntree's chest.

The older man groaned in pain and then in anger as he fell backward. But he jumped up quickly, before Joe could get away. He reached into the jeep and grabbed Joe's head from behind, and with all his strength, he slammed Joe's head into the steering wheel.

Joe fell on his stomach across the front seat of the jeep, rolling and holding his head.

Click. Click. Joe was too stunned at first to know what the sound was, but he could feel something tight on his wrists. As his head cleared he realized that Barntree had handcuffed his hands behind his back!

"Get out," Barntree barked, panting heavily. He pulled Joe out of the jeep by the handcuffs.

Joe's legs were shaking and wobbly, but his head was beginning to clear. Barntree pushed him up against the side of the jeep.

"Where's your brother?"

"He went to the movies," Joe said with half-open eyes.

The first slap across the face stunned Joe.

"Where's your brother?"

"He's watching TV reruns—he never misses them."

"Let's go, comedian," Barntree said. He

138

yanked on the handcuffs again, forcing Joe to walk.

"Where?" Joe asked.

"Right into the middle of the dump, that's where. You can stand in that ooze up to your neck until you glow in the dark," Barntree said. "Now that's something you can laugh about."

He pushed Joe one step and then another toward the tanker trucks and toward the toxic wastes.

"I've got your brother!" Barntree shouted to the woods. "You'd better give up, or he's taking a bath in my toxic wastes!"

"Let him go, Barntree!" shouted a voice that seemed to come from everywhere in the woods. It was Frank! "Let my brother go, and tell your truckers to stop unloading that junk!"

"I give the orders around here," Barntree shouted back. He was turning in a circle, trying to see where Frank was hiding. "I've been doing it for thirty years, and I'm not ready to stop."

"Don't listen, Frank!" Joe yelled.

"Stop the dumping and let Joe go, Barntree!" Frank shouted. His voice came from another direction this time.

"Don't you get it? I'm holding all the cards," Barntree said. "I've got your brother, and he's going to die if you don't do what I say."

"But I've got someone, too," Frank shouted back. "I've got your wife!"

139

15 Dangerous Deal

Barntree's eyes flashed with a combination of anger and fear. Joe had seen the man almost lose control of his temper once or twice in the past two days, but he had never seen Barntree look like this. The confidence that was the key to Barntree's power seemed to drain out of his face.

"What are you saying?" Barntree shouted into the woods.

Frank called again from somewhere else in the park. "I've got your wife. She's tied up somewhere in the woods. How long do you want her to stay outside tonight, Barntree?" The rancher didn't answer. "Tell the truckers to stop dumping those chemicals. And take the handcuffs off my brother—now!"

140

The truckers had become very still. Frank wondered if they were going to help Barntree— or just try to get out of the park before they got caught in the act of illegal dumping.

"You're just a kid," Barntree finally said halfheartedly.

"Yeah? Well, I had to do a lot of growing up tonight!" Frank yelled. "Let my brother go—or you'll never see your wife again!"

"I've never heard him talk like this," Joe said honestly. "You've pushed him too far, Barntree. He's over the edge."

"Okay, okay!" Barntree shouted. "I'm unlocking the cuffs." He reached into his pocket and fumbled for the key.

"No tricks!" Frank called back.

"Wait," Joe said when his hands were free. "Your jeep keys. Give me the keys to your jeep."

"What for? So you can run like a jackrabbit?" Barntree laughed. "I should have known you boys were too spineless to stick it out to the end."

"Are you free, Joe?" Frank shouted.

"Yeah!" Joe called to his brother.

"Cuff him!" Frank shouted back.

Joe didn't ask why. He just did what his brother asked him to do. That's what trusting each other was really all about.

He put the handcuffs on Barntree. It wasn't easy. Barntree kept moving, searching the forest with his eyes, trying to find where Frank had his wife. Then Joe snapped the cuffs shut and pulled on them once, hard, to make sure they were locked.

"Ouch," Barntree said. "What are the cuffs for, anyway?"

But the answer didn't come from Joe.

"Because you're going to be really mad when you find out that your wife is tied up in the basement of your ranch," Frank said, stepping out of the woods at last. "Our mom and dad didn't raise kidnappers," he added with a smile.

A look of complete self-disgust crossed Barntree's face. His eyes narrowed into slits, and he started to charge at Frank. But Joe tripped him, and he went down hard.

"Listen, Frank," Joe said, pointing toward the dump site. "The last tanker's finished pumping."

"You're too late," Barntree said smugly as he struggled to his feet.

Joe reached into Barntree's pocket and grabbed the jeep keys. "Maybe my plan will still work," he said. "Follow me, and bring Barntree over here!"

Joe ran for the jeep, jumped in, and started it. Then he drove it into position so that it blocked the opening in the fence. The tankers were trapped on the park side.

"You think that's going to stop these guys?" Barntree laughed. "They'll just drive the trucks right over that little thing."

"That'll be bad luck for you," Joe called, climbing out of the jeep. He ran over to Barntree and gave him a shove. "Because you're going to be sitting inside!"

Barntree stared at Joe. "You wouldn't dare—"

"It'll give you someplace to sit while we wait for the police," Frank interrupted, helping his brother push Barntree toward the jeep. But Barntree wouldn't get in.

"I forgot to tell him we called the police," Joe said.

"Where are they coming from? China?" Barntree said. "No one's coming. J. P. Arthur is *my* man."

Frank and Joe wondered if Barntree was right. Maybe the police *weren't* coming. Maybe Kwo hadn't understood that he was supposed to call the sheriff in Lawton, not Sheriff Arthur. It could be that Frank and Joe were waiting around for the law—and the wrong law was going to show up.

"Any minute now my drivers are going to wonder what's going on over here," Barntree said. "And when they do, they'll put you two out of commission in a hurry."

Joe glanced toward the dump site. Why hadn't the drivers come out of the woods? It was quiet— too quiet for Joe.

Just then a pair of headlights flashed into Frank's eyes. They were from a car, or maybe a truck, coming up the long private road that wound through Barntree's property.

"The police!" Frank said.

Barntree laughed. "If it's the police, why aren't they using their sirens or flashers?"

143

It was only one vehicle, and it was coming fast. When it skidded to a stop just inches from Barntree's jeep, Frank and Joe saw why there was no siren or flasher on top. It wasn't a police vehicle at all. It was Robbie McCoy's van with the Skeleton Rider painted on the side.

"Robbie!" Barntree said, and it almost sounded like a cheer.

Robbie McCoy opened his door and slipped out from behind the wheel.

"Would you look at me?" Barntree said with a laugh. "They've got me tied up like a steer. Get me out of these things."

"No way, Ben," Robbie said, shaking his head. "The police are on the way. I just came to make sure you didn't get out of this somehow, the way you've gotten out of everything else."

Frank and Joe were stunned. They didn't know whether to believe McCoy. Joe kept his guard up, ready to fight if this was some kind of trick.

"How did you know we called the police?" Frank asked cautiously.

"I was driving around, and I heard you on the CB with Becky's kid. I put two and two together —then I drove into town," Robbie explained.

But before Robbie could go on with his story, a siren and a flashing light pierced the night. Then a line of police cars quickly snaked through the dark on the winding road to the dump site.

Barntree struggled to get out of the handcuffs, trying to get away. He butted Joe with his shoulder and started to run. But Frank tackled him around the knees and brought him down, hitting the ground hard.

"Good evening," said a police officer walking toward them with his revolver drawn. "Officer Fresnell, Lawton Police."

"This isn't your jurisdiction," Barntree said, standing up and sounding very official. "You're in Axeblade now."

"This is my jurisdiction temporarily, since your police chief has been placed under arrest. I have him in the back of one of my cars. Are you Ben Barntree?" said the officer.

"Yes, I am, and I want you to arrest these kids," Barntree said, trying to put the old power back into his voice.

"Excuse me a minute," said Officer Fresnell. He lit a flare to signal the other police officers, who climbed out of four other cars. They followed Fresnell to the dump site, except for one officer who stayed behind, silently watching Frank, Joe, Robbie, and Barntree.

On his way back, Officer Fresnell checked out the tanker trucks. The drivers had gone.

"We've had a complaint of illegal toxic dumping in the national park," Officer Fresnell said. "It looks like the truck drivers have taken a sudden interest in hiking. But, Ben Barntree, I'm placing you under arrest," he said.

"Me?" Barntree said.

"Yes, sir. You, Sly Wilkins, and Phoenix Dawson," the officer said.

"Who filed this complaint? I want to know," Barntree insisted.

"I did," Robbie McCoy said.

Barntree roared with laughter. "You think you can walk away from this, Robbie? You're as dirty as anyone else."

"I know." Robbie had a pained expression on his face. "That's why I named myself in the complaint, too."

Just then two people got out of Officer Fresnell's squad car and came nearer—Becky and Kwo.

"Hey, Kwo!" Joe said. "You really came through."

"No big deal," said Kwo with a smile. "Math is one of my best subjects."

Becky looked happy, too. "Ben Barntree," she said, staring at him without a bit of forgiveness or fear, "I would have *crawled* all the way from town, just to see the police haul you away. I've been hoping for this for a long time—hoping you'd make a mistake."

"You're making the mistake, Rebecca," Barntree said in his usual cool way. But Becky didn't flinch.

"Officer," Frank said, "we have reason to believe this man murdered Tom Waldo, Becky Waldo's husband."

Becky put her arm around Kwo and pulled him close. "You can prove it? You can really prove it?" she asked Frank.

"He confessed to us," Frank told her. "And if we need more proof than that, we'll get it."

"There will be time to look into that later, ma'am," the officer interrupted. Then he focused on Frank and Joe. "Who are you two?"

"Frank Hardy."

"Joe Hardy."

"Okay. You're the ones Mrs. Waldo here told us about," he said. He wrote down Frank and Joe's names in his book. Then he turned to one of the other officers. "I think we should start putting people in cars and heading for the station, Officer Douglas."

"Excuse me, Officer," said Frank. "Can I ask one quick question?"

Officer Fresnell nodded.

"We saw a letter in your van about diverting water from the Canary River," Frank said to Robbie. "What was that about?"

"I was looking for another source of water for my cattle," Robbie said.

"Why?" said Joe.

"Because I didn't want to get my water from the Ruby River anymore," Robbie said.

"Why not? You knew it wasn't polluted," Frank said.

"Yeah, I knew," Robbie said. "I remembered my dad always told me to keep on good terms with Barntree, 'cause the Ruby River was fed by an underground spring on his land. So I figured out if Ben went ahead and used his land for the

147

toxic dump, it would kill the Ruby. I told Sly and Phoenix because we all have ranches that live and die by the water supply."

"None of this is true," Barntree said.

"Just let me talk, Ben. For once, just let me talk," Robbie said. "We went to Ben and told him what we knew. But he had already signed too many contracts, and a lot of money was going to come his way from companies that needed to get rid of their chemical wastes. So Ben came up with the idea of dumping the stuff in the park. And he paid us to keep our mouths shut."

"The letter?" Frank asked again.

"I was trying not to use the Ruby anymore. I wanted to get clear of Ben," Robbie said.

"That's more than one question," Officer Fresnell said. "Let's go hear the rest of this in Axeblade. It's going to be a long night."

"I've got plenty of coffee at the café," Becky offered. Then she came over to Frank and Joe with a smile. "Thanks."

"It's not over," Frank said. "At least not about your husband's death."

"It's over for Axeblade," she said. "You guys did what a whole town didn't have the nerve to do."

"Aw, shucks. It was nothin', ma'am," Joe said with a Western twang. "We just had some time to kill till our van was fixed, that's all."

Frank, Becky, and Kwo all laughed.

"Speaking of our van, I wonder how Bill Hunt is doing with it," Frank said.

But Frank and Joe didn't get to Bill Hunt's garage until late the next afternoon. Officer Fresnell kept them busy all morning. They told him everything they'd learned and answered all his questions. Then they had to give their statements over again while an officer took it all down in shorthand.

As they walked down the dusty street, warm in the late-afternoon sun, Frank said, "Things have changed here."

"Yeah, people are saying hello to us and smiling," said Joe.

Axeblade Pete came running up. The old man had brushed his bushy beard and put on an old-fashioned white shirt and string tie. "My friends," the old man said to anyone who'd listen, "if you elect me sheriff, you'll never have to buy me another meal—unless you really want to. Elect an honest sheriff. I'm honest as the day is long, even in winter when the days get short."

"Save it for the voters of Axeblade," Frank said. "Joe and I are on our way back to Bayport."

"Don't forget to write," the old man said with a wink. "You know, I've forgotten how to write twice. Had to teach myself from scratch."

Frank and Joe laughed, shook hands with Axeblade Pete, and said goodbye.

Then Frank and Joe walked down to Bill Hunt's garage to pick up their van.

"Yo, Bill!" Joe called.

"Hey, how'd it go?" Bill asked, looking a little nervous.

"I think this case will have a very happy ending," Joe said. "Barntree's racked up a pretty good list of charges against him, including federal charges because of the national park. The FBI's been called in to find out who else was involved, from what I hear."

"Well, we're gonna miss you big-city guys," the mechanic said.

"Hey, you were a big-city guy once—UCLA," Frank said. "Why'd you ever come back here?"

"L.A. was not for me. Too noisy and too much pollution—isn't that a laugh?" Bill Hunt said.

"Yeah," Joe said.

"Listen, I'm sorry I didn't help you guys out more," Bill said, looking off into the distance. "I wanted to, but I just couldn't do something against my sister. You know what I mean?"

"Sometimes it's tough," said Joe. "So how's our van?"

"It's not quite done yet, guys," Bill Hunt said quickly.

"What exactly isn't quite done?" asked Frank.

"Well, I haven't exactly installed the water pump yet," Bill Hunt said.

"It's been five days!" Frank said.

The garage mechanic smiled. "I'm still waiting for the parts," he said. "Nobody said *everything* in Axeblade was going to change!"

THE HARDY BOYS® SERIES
By Franklin W. Dixon

Title	Code	Price	
NIGHT OF THE WEREWOLF—#59	62480	$3.50	_____
MYSTERY OF THE SAMURAI SWORD—#60	67302	$3.50	_____
THE PENTAGON SPY—#61	67221	$3.50	_____
THE APEMAN'S SECRET—#62	62479	$3.50	_____
THE MUMMY CASE—#63	64289	$3.50	_____
MYSTERY OF SMUGGLERS COVE—#64	66229	$3.50	_____
THE STONE IDOL—#65	62626	$3.50	_____
THE VANISHING THIEVES—#66	63890	$3.50	_____
THE OUTLAW'S SILVER—#67	64285	$3.50	_____
DEADLY CHASE—#68	62477	$3.50	_____
THE FOUR-HEADED DRAGON—#69	65797	$3.50	_____
THE INFINITY CLUE—#70	62475	$3.50	_____
TRACK OF THE ZOMBIE—#71	62623	$3.50	_____
THE VOODOO PLOT—#72	64287	$3.50	_____
THE BILLION DOLLAR RANSOM—#73	66228	$3.50	_____
TIC-TAC-TERROR—#74	66858	$3.50	_____
TRAPPED AT SEA—#75	64290	$3.50	_____
GAME PLAN FOR DISASTER—#76	64288	$3.50	_____
THE CRIMSON FLAME—#77	64286	$3.50	_____
SKY SABOTAGE—#79	62625	$3.50	_____
THE ROARING RIVER MYSTERY—#80	63823	$3.50	_____
THE DEMON'S DEN—#81	62622	$3.50	_____
THE BLACKWING PUZZLE—#82	62624	$3.50	_____
THE SWAMP MONSTER—#83	49727	$3.50	_____
REVENGE OF THE DESERT PHANTOM—#84	49729	$3.50	_____
SKYFIRE PUZZLE—#85	49731	$3.50	_____
THE MYSTERY OF THE SILVER STAR—#86	64374	$3.50	_____
PROGRAM FOR DESTRUCTION—#87	64895	$3.50	_____
TRICKY BUSINESS—#88	64973	$3.50	_____
THE SKY BLUE FRAME—#89	64974	$3.50	_____
DANGER ON THE DIAMOND—#90	63425	$3.50	_____
SHIELD OF FEAR—#91	66308	$3.50	_____
THE SHADOW KILLERS—#92	66309	$3.50	_____
THE BILLION DOLLAR RANSOM—#93	66310	$3.50	_____
BREAKDOWN IN AXEBLADE—#94	66311	$3.50	_____
THE HARDY BOYS® GHOST STORIES	50808	$3.50	_____
NANCY DREW® AND THE HARDY BOYS® SUPER SLEUTHS	43375	$3.50	_____
NANCY DREW® AND THE HARDY BOYS® SUPER SLEUTHS #2	50194	$3.50	_____

NANCY DREW® and THE HARDY BOYS® are trademarks of Simon & Schuster,
registered in the United States Patent and Trademark Office.

AND DON'T FORGET...NANCY DREW CASEFILES® NOW AVAILABLE IN PAPERBACK.

NANCY DREW® MYSTERY STORIES
By Carolyn Keene

	ORDER NO.	PRICE	QUANTITY
THE TRIPLE HOAX—#57	64278	$3.50	
THE FLYING SAUCER MYSTERY—#58	65796	$3.50	
THE SECRET IN THE OLD LACE—#59	63822	$3.50	
THE GREEK SYMBOL MYSTERY—#60	67457	$3.50	
THE SWAMI'S RING—#61	62467	$3.50	
THE KACHINA DOLL MYSTERY—#62	67220	$3.50	
THE TWIN DILEMMA—#63	67301	$3.50	
CAPTIVE WITNESS—#64	62469	$3.50	
MYSTERY OF THE WINGED LION—#65	62681	$3.50	
RACE AGAINST TIME—#66	62476	$3.50	
THE SINISTER OMEN—#67	62471	$3.50	
THE ELUSIVE HEIRESS—#68	62478	$3.50	
CLUE IN THE ANCIENT DISGUISE—#69	64279	$3.50	
THE BROKEN ANCHOR—#70	62481	$3.50	
THE SILVER COBWEB—#71	62470	$3.50	
THE HAUNTED CAROUSEL—#72	66227	$3.50	
ENEMY MATCH—#73	64283	$3.50	
MYSTERIOUS IMAGE—#74	64284	$3.50	
THE EMERALD-EYED CAT MYSTERY—#75	64282	$3.50	
THE ESKIMO'S SECRET—#76	62468	$3.50	
THE BLUEBEARD ROOM—#77	66857	$3.50	
THE PHANTOM OF VENICE—#78	66230	$3.50	
THE DOUBLE HORROR OF FENLEY PLACE—#79	64387	$3.50	
THE CASE OF THE DISAPPEARING DIAMONDS—#80	64896	$3.50	
MARDI GRAS MYSTERY—#81	64961	$3.50	
THE CLUE IN THE CAMERA—#82	64962	$3.50	
THE CASE OF THE VANISHING VEIL—#83	63413	$3.50	
THE JOKER'S REVENGE—#84	63426	$3.50	
THE SECRET OF SHADY GLEN—#85	63416	$3.50	
THE MYSTERY OF MISTY CANYON—#86	63417	$3.50	
THE CASE OF THE RISING STARS—#87	66312	$3.50	
NANCY DREW® GHOST STORIES—#1	46468	$3.50	
NANCY DREW® GHOST STORIES—#2	55070	$3.50	
NANCY DREW® AND THE HARDY BOYS® SUPER SLEUTHS	43375	$3.50	
NANCY DREW® AND THE HARDY BOYS® SUPER SLEUTHS #2	50194	$3.50	

and don't forget...THE HARDY BOYS® Now available in paperback

Simon & Schuster, Mail Order Dept. ND5
200 Old Tappan Road, Old Tappan, NJ 07675
Please send me copies of the books checked. (If not completely satisfied, return for full refund in 14 days.)

☐ Enclosed full amount per copy with this coupon
(Send check or money order only.)
Please be sure to include proper postage and handling:
95¢—first copy
50¢—each additonal copy ordered.

☐ If order is for $10.00 or more,
you may charge to one of the
following accounts:
☐ Mastercard ☐ Visa

Name _____ Credit Card No. _____

Address _____

City _____ Card Expiration Date _____

State _____ Zip _____ Signature _____

Books listed are also available at your local bookstore. Prices are subject to change without notice.

Murder Ink.® Mysteries

Scene Of The Crime® Mysteries